Uncle Ned

Stories, as read out on
BBC Radio Merseyside

Written and illustrated by
Douglas Griffiths

Text and images by Douglas Griffiths

First Published 2014 by Appin Press, an imprint of Countyvise Ltd
14 Appin Road, Birkenhead, CH41 9HH

British Library Cataloguing in Publication Data.
A catalogue record for this book is available from the British Library.

ISBN: 978-1-910352-05-2

About the author

Douglas Griffiths was born in 1933 and grew up in Tranmere, part of the Wirral town of Birkenhead, which faces across the River Mersey to Liverpool. Living in the shadow of the great Cammell Laird shipyard, where his father worked and where he was to work himself for part of his career, the young Douglas got to know very well the people and characters of this rough but friendly working-class district. Birkenhead, with its docks and industry, was badly bombed during the Second World War, but its people remained defiant and full of humour. Tranmere was still a close-knit community throughout the post-war decades, where people knew all of their neighbours, gossiped about their business, and looked out for each other. It was a time when you could leave your front door open, because few had anything worth stealing. The shipyard is now a shadow of its former self, the grimy railway yards and old factories have been replaced by McDonalds and other plastic, impersonal signs of modern life, and the community is no longer quite so close-knit. However the memories remain. Many of the steep streets of terraced housing survive, and even one or two of the old pubs are still there – not quite as dark, smoky, and crowded with thirsty working men just off shift as they once were, but still serving pints.

Douglas has lived in Heswall, on the leafier western side of the Wirral Peninsula overlooking the River Dee, since getting married and starting a family in the mid-1960s. His writing has mainly been poetry and humorous stories about old Wirral characters. He has also published several articles on sailing themes in 'Practical Boatowner' and other yachting magazines. Uncle Ned is familiar to listeners of BBC Radio Merseyside, where some of these stories were narrated by the late Colin Bean (best known as 'Private Sponge' from the BBC hit comedy Dad's Army), and to many people involved in Wirral writers' workshops over the years.

To Enid

Contents

The wine tasting

'Uncle Ned, A Man of many Parts'

Uncle Ned was a pragmatist; not that he would put it quite that way himself, nor would it be advisable to tell him so, not after what happened to Charlie the postman who, by the way, considered himself a man of letters. He called Uncle Ned a chauvinist one night in the 'Boilermakers Arms'. Charlie was correct in what he said but unfortunately failed to foresee that the retired shipyard worker might misunderstand his meaning. Ned was on his fifth or sixth pint at the time.

However, it was generally agreed that not much harm had been done. The furnishings in the pub needed replacing anyway, and Charlie was soon back on his round with scarcely any sign of a limp.

Auntie Elsie would have agreed that Uncle Ned was a chauvinist, if she knew what it meant, which she probably did, come to think of it, as she had been to night school. She had been to literary appreciation classes run by the local Townswomen's Guild.

Ned's interest in books did not extend beyond those books on horse racing form, a subject on which he was something of an expert. When Elsie mentioned D.H. Lawrence he thought she meant 'That Army bloke who used to dress up as an Arab.'

Ned was also a hypochondriac, another description which, if applied to Ned directly, would be likely to have painful consequences. He would never take a holiday in case the water disagreed with him, which is surprising as he seldom drank any. Before he retired he always told Elsie that he wasn't entitled to holidays. When pressed on the subject he admitted that his firm had offered him some time off in lieu but, as he said,' Who the 'eck wants to go to Cornwall at this time o' year?' He had also been advised that he could take his holidays at his own convenience, which he felt to be equally unhelpful.

After his retirement, he had no such excuses but still managed to avoid taking Auntie Elsie out anywhere. When she dropped subtle hints such as, 'Isn't it about time we went on a coach trip or something?' He would play on his occupational deafness, which was real enough, but not so severe that he failed to hear the racing results, or the offer of a drink in the 'Boilermakers Arms'. If this strategy failed, which, with Auntie Elsie it usually did, he would become very forgetful. He always protested that he had taken Elsie to the pictures, 'not very long ago,' but he could never remember the name of the film. Whenever Ned got an attack of convenient forgetfulness Elsie would remember something about cooking with aluminium pans being a possible cause of memory loss. She would shake her head and say 'I must get rid of them aluminium pans.'

In addition to all that, Ned was an optimist. He did the pools every week hoping to repeat his one and only win of ten pounds, many years before. He had been drunk for a week. He was wild in those days. So was Auntie Elsie when she found he'd spent the lot. Auntie Elsie reckoned the pools were an expensive way to play noughts and crosses.

From time to time Auntie Elsie tried to involve Ned in more civilised pursuits than those that took place in the 'Boilermakers Arms', namely darts and dominoes, not to mention the occasional discussion that all too often each party flatly contradicting the other, then casting doubts on the other's intelligence, then on the others ancestry.

Elsie's path to self-improvement lay through the Townswomen's Guild where she learned a variety of social skills including flower arranging, keep fit and continental cooking. The results of the latter did not go down well with Uncle Ned.

Some of the Guild meetings were open to husbands and other guests but Ned was aghast at the slightest suggestion of his attending. He absolutely refused to go to a lecture on local history, which, he declared, he had heard all about from his Grandfather. He said 'The goings-on in them days are no fit subject for a women's club.' Nor was he interested in gardening. His long-ago attempt to grow potatoes on an allotment was a total failure. Elsie reckoned he had planted them upside down.

One day, Elsie asked Ned to go with her to a wine-tasting evening at the Guild. Ned's attitude then became one of crafty speculation. 'I might just manage that one, luv,' he said, 'I always reckon 'usbands and wives should do things together.' Elsie cast him a glance full of disbelief. 'As long as I don't 'ave to eat that paella stuff again,' he continued. 'You always bring that up' replied Elsie. But it was obvious that she was pleased.

The meeting started well. The speaker described the characteristics of a range of table wines from sweet white through to dry red. He explained that a good wine need not be expensive as it all depended on 'the quality of the grapes'. He repeated this phrase several times. He also stressed that all the wines he recommended could be obtained at very reasonable cost at the Kut Kost supermarket.

'This is a bloomin' advertising stunt,' muttered Ned, shifting his feet impatiently. 'When do we get to taste the stuff?' Ned's question was answered when the speaker's assistant began to pass around samples of the wine. Immediately he was at the front with urgent questions such as, 'what do you mean by dry? It looks wet enough to me,' and 'What do you mean by bouquet? I don't see any flowers?'

He was about to the purpose of the plastic bowls on the floor until one of the more cultured-looking visitors took a mouthful of wine, made a gargling noise and spat it in the bowl. 'Blimey!' exclaimed Ned, 'that one can't be much good.'

The speaker did not appear to resent Uncle Ned's philistine approach but set about instructing him in the art of wine appreciation, drinking several glasses in the process. Ned too drank several glasses in the interests of learning, of course, and could soon tell a claret from a sauvignon blanc.

A scene of great conviviality soon developed with much laughter. Bottles of sparkling wine were being uncorked with a sound like an artillery barrage.

The ladies of the Guild were not amused. Many of them wanted to ask the speaker questions but found him being monopolised by Ned like some old crony. What's more, the speaker was becoming incoherent, rambling on about 'the colity of the gapes'.

It was quite obvious that the meeting would have to be cut short.

After the speaker had been carried out an ugly scene developed. Ned, by then tipsy, made an attempt to take over the lecture. A wall of hostile women advanced toward the platform. Elsie, showing great presence of mind, as well amazing strength, frog-marched Ned out of the room.

By the time she got him home he was distinctly glassy-eyed and rubber-legged. Her tirade about him, 'showing her up' and, 'never taking him into respectable company again' was largely wasted. He stared at the wall with a horrified expression, not really listening.

'Did you see 'em?' he slurred. 'It was like in that picture I took you to see not long ago, you know that one with Stanley Baker in it, and that other young feller, Michael Caine. 'That must have been a long time ago', put in Elsie, acidly. But Ned was not listening. 'No more women's clubs for me,' he declared, shuddering. 'I'd sooner face the flippin' Zulus'.

Another thing about Ned; he was a born survivor.

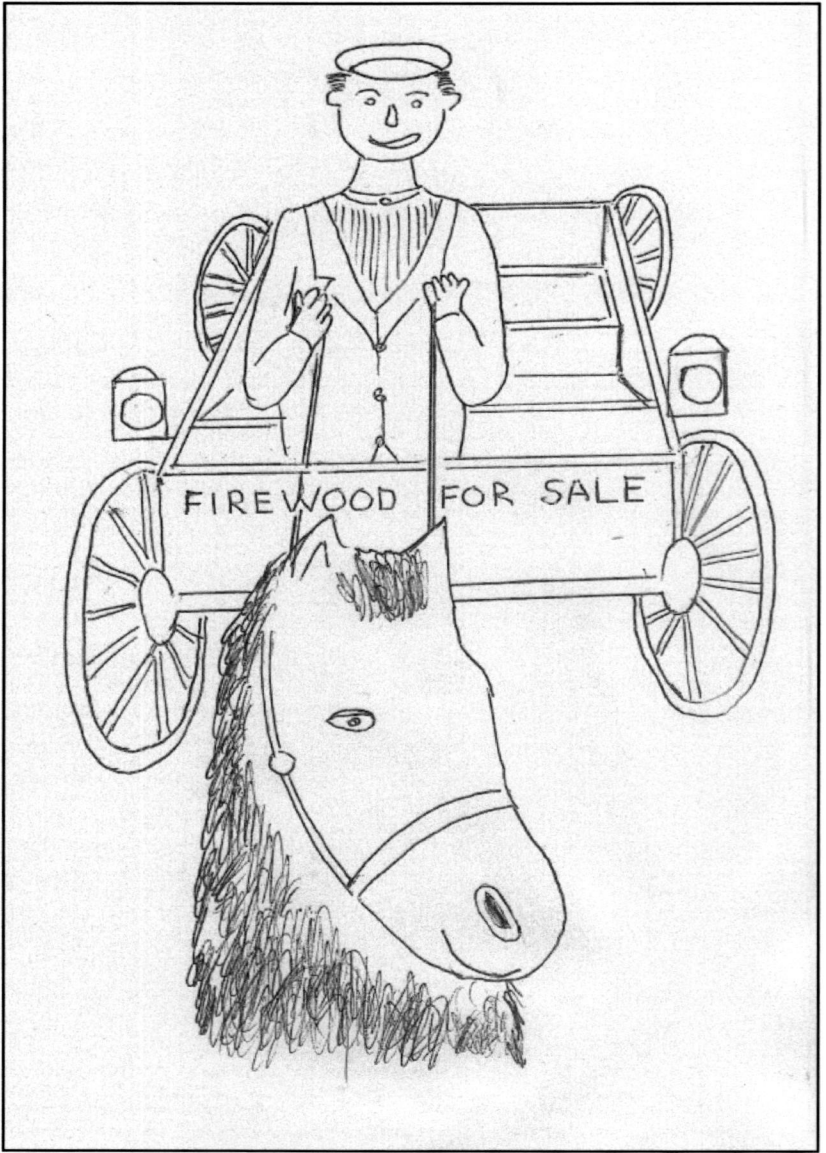

Ready for the off

'A Day at the Races'

Uncle Ned was a compulsive gambler. His speciality was the horses. He was known throughout the district, that warren of old property between the shipyard and the bottom road, as an expert. Men came from far and wide to the 'Boilermaker's Arms', Ned's favourite pub, for advice. Many returned for more advice after the failure of the first, apparently undeterred by the appearance of the expert, a retired shipyard worker in flat cap and muffler.

Auntie Elsie never ceased to be amazed at their faith. She declared that she and Ned could have retired in luxury years ago if even half of Ned's certainties had won. More cynically, she said that Ned, if he had won a fortune, would have bought a pub and locked himself in.

As she often said, she had only herself to blame. As a girl she could have married the richest young man in the district, the pawnbroker's son. Unfortunately, when he produced an engagement ring, she recognised it as her grandmother's.

One thing Ned could not be called was mean; even though he was often broke. This could not be explained entirely by the smallness of his pension. As Auntie Elsie said he had often been broke even when he had been earning good money by hammering rivets into the side of ships. However, being broke never depressed Ned. One of his favourite expressions was, 'Never mind, eh'

He always had big ideas for getting rich, most of which would have made the South Sea Bubble look like a sound business proposition.

Not that he ever set out to rob anyone; usually it was Ned who ended up robbed. He was like that, as Elsie put it: exasperating. When they had been newlywed, Elsie had thought that she could cure him but a few early episodes made her realise that he was incurable. As an example she told the story of Ned's extraordinary trip to Chester Races.

The year was 1939, the last summer of the uneasy peace. Although the shipyard was busy building ships for the war everyone knew was coming, the district was still poverty-stricken from years of slump; overcrowded too. That was before wartime bombing and post-war clearance opened it up and, in some opinions, destroyed most of its colourful character.

One of the great traditions of the district was a once-a-year visit to the City of Chester for the annual horse racing. Early in the morning of the long-awaited day there would be a mass exodus by excursion train or motor coaches known as "charas". Fares were cheap, but not cheap enough for everybody; many were left behind

Ned's idea was to compete with the charas using a horse-drawn vehicle, a wagonette. By the nineteen thirties this was a very obsolete form of transport and most of them had been cut up for firewood. However the old man who owned the woodyard opposite the 'Boilermakers Arms' had one in fairly usable condition and was willing to hire it out together with his horse. Ned had not needed much persuading even though the horse had more corners than a hat-stand. 'Do you think the horse could pull us to Chester and back?' he had asked, speculatively. 'As sure as I could beat Jack Johnson' replied the old man.

Taking that as agreement, Ned went ahead and booked a full load of customers for the return trip. As most of them could not afford to travel either by chara or by train, the payment was mostly either 'on delivery' or 'on account', the latter being the reckless understanding that they would pay out of their winnings

Some of Ned's cronies were inclined to scoff at the scheme, especially young 'Arry Wade the landlord's son from the 'Boilermaker's Arms'. Remarks about 'cat's meat' were quickly discouraged by Ned. Young 'Arry was no hero. He seemed to live in fear of the local hard characters, especially one known as 'Big Norman'. Young 'Arry reckoned that Big Norman would be busy among the home going crowds extorting money from those who had any. He seemed to think he'd be safer on the train, as he said, 'There are no communication cords on charas.'

When the day of the races came there was great excitement. Ned had got up early so as to start in plenty of time. He looked an important figure up on the driving seat, shaking the reins impatiently. Unfortunately some of his passengers did not have the same sense of urgency. One of them, an elderly man of similar build to the horse, arrived after the wagonette had started. He had to catch it up by running after it, which he did quite easily.

The horse however, was stronger than it looked, being used daily to pull a two-wheeled cart loaded with firewood up steep hills. It settled to a steady five miles an hour and looked set to keep it up all day.

When they reached the first pub, the passengers decided among themselves, unanimously, to stop for a drink. Ned, being young at the time, was rather surprised that passengers who could not pay their fares could afford to buy drinks. As stopping at every pub to rest the horse was an important part of the tradition, Ned had little option but to join in the spirit of the occasion. No doubt he needed very little persuasion, as Auntie Elsie put it.

After the stopping procedure had been repeated several times, the wagonette arrived at the racecourse just in time for the big race of the day. The passengers, by now in jovial mood were quite unconcerned and, once inside the racecourse, checked the locations of essential services, notably the beer tent.

Ned, left to his own devices, spent his remaining money on a few small bets, none of which were successful. He then fell in with Young 'Arry and a few other cronies who were, by contrast, flushed with success.

In spite of this, Young 'Arry seemed very nervous. He kept glancing around and asking if anyone had seen Big Norman. He told Ned that he intended to leave as soon as the last race finished and catch the first available train home. Ned offered Young 'Arry a lift home for his own safety, which Young 'Arry declined, not very graciously, making further scornful remarks about Ned's vehicle. Ned was stung by this lack of gratitude, so much so that he made a foolish bet that he would get home before Young 'Arry, five pounds to be paid by the loser to the winner.

'Five pounds?' repeated Elsie in outraged tones, 'more than a week's wages.' It certainly looked as though Ned's five pounds was lost forever when the wagonette arrived home. By the time it crawled in, it was near to midnight. The driver, the passengers and the horse were all the worse for wear. The cart itself looked worse of all with its offside wheels wobbling dangerously and the side boarding all splintered.

It seemed that Ned, in a spirited attempt to win his impulsive and virtually unwinnable bet, had coaxed the old horse into a brief gallop. Unfortunately this had occurred in the city centre traffic with the result that they collided with a motorcar. Not an ordinary motorcar either but one with a crest on the door and a flag on the bonnet. Luckily, nobody had been hurt.

The next day Ned was very downcast. He was suffering from a hangover that was not improved by Auntie Elsie's severe criticism regarding the foolish bet; foolish being one of her milder descriptions of Ned's conduct.

Needless to say, Ned kept well away from the 'Boilermaker's Arms,' so it was late in the day before he happened to meet Young 'Arry, an event he had been dreading. His pocket cash was well short of five pounds; five shillings was about its present level.

To Ned's surprise, Young 'Arry showed no sign of jubilation. He just muttered something about 'Might have been better to have travelled on your ramshackle cart after all,' and thrust five pounds into Ned's hand.

Understandably, Ned was puzzled by this and questioned Young 'Arry about how he could have arrived by train even later than the wagonette. It seemed that Big Norman and his gang had boarded the same train that Young 'Arry had caught. It seemed that Big Norman must have decided that the first train home would provide the best pickings but this strategy had one drawback; the earlier home goers had more money than the later ones but, being less drunk were less inclined to part with it in exchange for not being given a taste of Big Norman's knuckleduster.

A large-scale fight had broken out; somebody had pulled the communication cord and the Police had boarded the train at a halfway station. By the time everything was sorted out it had been very late indeed.

Ned went around the local area in a state of triumph. He waved his five pound note in Elsie's face and demanded to know, 'Who's foolish now, eh?' He waved his money in other people's faces while the money lasted, which it didn't for long once he had settled himself in the 'Boilermaker's Arms'.

The next day Ned was as broke as ever. The fares of his wagonette passengers, those few that paid at all, scarcely covered the hire of the horse. Ned took it all philosophically as usual. 'Never mind, eh,' just about summed it up as far as he was concerned.

Auntie Elsie did not share this view at all. She was not at all pleased, especially when, a few days later, Ned had to attend court at Chester and was convicted of driving without due care and attention.

They fined him five pounds.

The weightlifter

'Heroes One and All.'

Uncle Ned was a man of many parts, impression that grew on me gradually. He would deny any suggestion to this effect with assertion that he was, 'an ordinary bloke.'

However, some of his tales give different impression. He had not long left school at the age of fourteen when he persuaded his first employer, a scrap-wood merchant to lend him a horse and cart so that he could take fare-paying passengers to Chester Races.

The fact that the trip was a financial dead loss and almost a disaster did not detract from the pattern that followed most of Ned's later escapades.

The days that followed the Chester trip were full of uncertainty. By the summer of 1939 the likelihood of war seemed stronger every day. People were worried. Mrs Wade, the wife of the landlord at 'The Boilermaker's Arms' was worried about bombs falling from the sky 'like rain'.

Her husband, 'Arry Wade was worried about the loss of his trade if his customers had to spend every night in air raid shelters. His son, 'Young 'Arry' was worried about being called up to fight for King and Country although the gloom of that prospect was lightened somewhat when he heard that the man who ran the scrap wood business was even more worried. 'What if they drop fire bombs? The whole woodyard would go up like a bonfire'.

Uncle Ned, after casual work at the woodyard, and jobs 'on the side' as errand boy or bookies runner, now had his future assured. Soon, he could start as an apprentice riveter at the shipyard. He'd had it confirmed. It meant he would be in a reserved occupation: safe from call-up for the next five years. He was not worried.

Young 'Arry confided to Ned that he, 'Could do with a few boxing lessons - too many hard cases around, There were two in the pub last night, causing trouble.' 'Did you throw 'em out?' asked Ned. 'No, me Mam did' was the answer.

'Hm, see what you mean.' Ned frowned disapprovingly. 'Can't you get your Dad to help? Hasn't he got a gymnastic - er - keep-fit room over the pub?'

'Yeah, but he doesn't do boxing, only weight-lifting, as if he doesn't lift enough barrels at his work.' 'Let's go and see if the old bloke at the woodyard can help,' suggested Ned. 'He told me he used to box when he was a lad.' 'That must have been a long time ago.' said 'Arry. 'Come on,' said Ned. 'It's worth a try.'

When they arrived at the woodyard the old man was repairing the cart damaged when Ned had borrowed it for the Chester trip. He was not in a good mood. 'Boxing eh?' He said wheezily. 'I boxed with Jack Johnson'.

'Wasn't he a heavyweight?' asked Ned. 'Of course, he was world champion.' 'But you're not as big as I am', said Ned, tactlessly. 'I didn't say I fought him,' was the angry reply. 'It was an exhibition bout when I was in the army in the last war. I was bigger then.' 'I thought you were a professional,' said Ned. 'I was,' replied the old man indignantly. 'I fought the Australian champion, Jake Studgett, "The Whistling Wallaby". What the 'ell are you laughing at? Come on, put 'em up!'

Ned, suddenly serious, stared at the skinny, crouching figure. He felt a stinging smack on his ear. Angrily, he tried to return the blow and got a lightning-fast smack on the other ear. He had not seen either coming. It occurred to him that had his jaw been the target he would not be standing rubbing his ear. 'Don't just stand there,' said the old man. 'Use your feet.'

'What, kick?' asked Ned, suddenly respectful. 'No, dance and duck, keep moving in other words, you great lump' He danced forward, skinny arm jabbing like a snake's tongue. 'Got to go, see you later' said Ned. He broke into a run, closely followed by 'Arry.

'That was a waste of time' said 'Arry when they were safely down the road. 'Oh I don't know' replied Ned. 'At least you know what you're up against.' 'Do you reckon that woodyard bloke was a professional?' asked 'Arry. 'I doubt it' replied Ned. 'Not a proper professional. He told me he used to fight with bare knuckles for bets on the shore fields.' 'Arry shuddered. 'Let's do some weight training at me Dad's gym.'

The gym was in a room over the pub where the locals had gathered for their Saturday night pint. It was separated from the bedroom by a crude wall of bricks. Old 'Arry was stripped to his singlet, lifting a loaded barbell with much puffing and blowing. He seemed pleased that his son had come to train of his own accord. Putting lighter weights on another bar he gave it to him to lift, which he did with a struggle but only shoulder high.

Meanwhile the noise from the pub below was increasing. Some of the older men were boasting about their war service and singing the songs of the trenches. There were shouts of, 'Let 'em all come.' The situation was getting out of hand. Mrs Wade sent a message up to her husband for support. She had rung the bell for last orders some time before but nobody would leave. They clamoured for more ale.

Old 'Arry got halfway down the stairs when there was an appalling crash. Ned had tried his strength with the heavier barbell, got it above his head, then lost control of it. It crashed through the floorboards, fortunately jamming in the joists. Even so it brought much of the plaster down. Bricks from the makeshift wall cascaded through the hole.

Ned, white as a sheet, stared at the mess. 'I'm sorry, Mrs Wade', he gasped. Old 'Arry took it better than had been expected. 'At least it cleared the pub', he said. 'They thought the war had started – ran like bloomin' rabbits, the lot of them.'

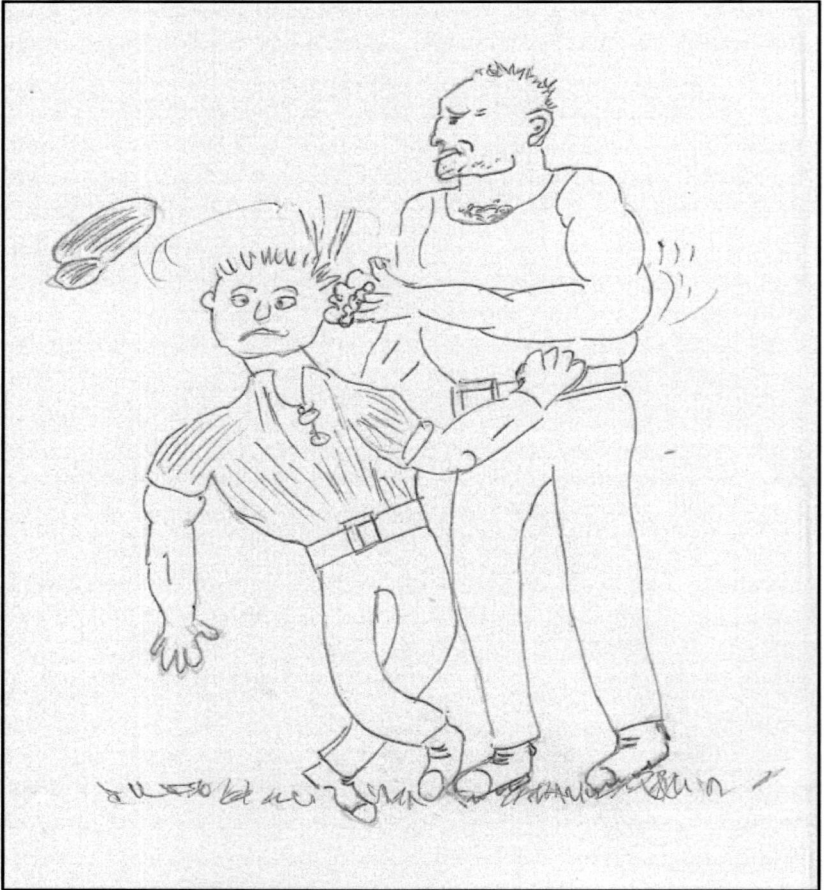

The fight with Big Norman

'Roll out the Barrel'

Auntie Elsie had spent half a lifetime trying to reform Uncle Ned. She had a vision of a more cultured lifestyle that had its beginning before she married Ned, when she refused a proposal of marriage from the wealthiest young man in the district, the pawnbroker's son.

Over the years she had remembered that episode in her life with some regret, especially when Ned indulged in the drink too freely or gambled too recklessly. Since his retirement from his job as a shipyard riveter, these lapses were controlled by lack of money and so became comparatively rare.

Elsie seemed content to attend meetings of the Townswomen's Guild, learn about such self-improving skills as creative homemaking, and make the most of Ned's few social graces. Occasionally, when so inclined, Elsie would tell tales of Ned's wilder youthful days when he had worked hard and played harder. To her these episodes were disgraceful but, in the context of the times they were perhaps not so extraordinary. One such tale concerned what happened on V.E. Day, 1945.

Ned's hostelry, then as now, was the 'Boilermaker's Arms' along the bottom road, conveniently, close to the shipyard. The landlord at that time was Old 'Arry Wade, father of the present licencee. With memories of Armistice Day 1918, Old 'Arry prepared for exceptional business demands.

When the day came it was, 'all hands to the pumps'. Uncle

Ned was in the forefront of the throng and, with a back pocketful of overtime pay he could afford to drink an impressive total of pints by early afternoon.

To get home from the 'Boilermaker's Arms', Ned had to walk up a steep hill. It seemed he was able to regulate his intake of ale so that he could still manage the climb; but it could be a very close calculation. Sometimes he was seen staggering in a zig-zag manner, side to side, three steps up and two steps down like in some slow-motion dance. At such times, Elsie kept behind her lace curtain.

However, on that memorable day, he arrived safely for his afternoon nap on the sofa before rising for his tea, of stewed oxtail, after which he was ready for the evening session.

By the time the street parties were over and the trestle tables cleared away, the evening's events at the 'Boilermaker's Arms' were just getting into their stride. As darkness fell the bonfires were lit on the bombsites. This caused some anxiety to the proprietor of the woodyard who spent half of the evening downing pints and the other half standing by with a stirrup pump while sparks drifted across his property and fireworks exploded in the sky. He said it was worse than the blitz, more like the battle of the Somme. He also said he would rather spar six rounds with Jack Johnson than go through that again.

At the 'Boilermaker's Arms', Old 'Arry was pulling pints with furious speed, assisted by Young 'Arry. Even Ned was co-opted as a glass collector, even though he was swaying like a tightrope walker who'd lost his balancing stick. By this time the company was very convivial, until an argument broke out between the shipyard workers and some service men off an American ship that was in for repairs. The latter claimed they had won the war and protected the lives of civilians who had enjoyed an easy time. Elsie wasn't sure what happened next but the furnishings in the pub were never the same again.

After the servicemen had left to go to 'a better place', which was a wise move on their part as they were in danger of going to 'a far better place', the company broke up into quarrelling groups. Old 'Arry Wade wanted to know who was going to pay for the damage. His customers declared that 'other lot' were to blame, whereupon Old 'Arry put the towels on the pumps and called time. The roar of disapproval could be heard half way up the hill, even though it was long gone normal closing time.

Auntie Elsie waited to see what sort of state Ned would arrive in. By the time he did turn up the dawn was rising over the shipyard. Elsie, stiff from sleeping in a chair, rose quickly nevertheless, grabbed Ned and turned his face towards the light. He was not a pretty sight. He had blood smeared around his nose, lips like sausages and one eye swollen shut. 'You been falling?' she asked, half concerned, half disgusted. 'No.' She added after a second look. 'Fighting?'

It was no use denying. In any case Ned was too exhausted to think of any lies. He had agreed to fight another man on the traditional early morning battling ground, the shore fields. His opponent had been Big Norman, a notorious thug.

'Serves you right,' said Elsie, 'I thought you'd have more sense. He's twice your size and twice as ugly – got more scars than a twelve-year-old tomcat.'

'I'd have given him a few more scars if he hadn't used a knuckleduster,' replied Ned. After saying this he collapsed and Elsie carried him upstairs in a fireman's lift, his boots clonking on every step.

Later in the day Elsie went down the hill to the bottom road. There were few people about, as though the frenzied rejoicing of the previous day had exhausted everyone. By coincidence, as Elsie reached the end of a row of shops, Big Norman came out of the alley where he lived and began to stroll along the pavement in his usual strutting way, thumbs hooked in his waistcoat pockets, his bleak gaze a clear signal to anyone in his way to get out of it, which they usually did. Elsie didn't. She picked up a piece of board from someone's fence that happened to be lying in the gutter, and battered Big Norman with it. Taken by surprise, he retreated in disarray, back down the alley. His reputation in the district was never quite the same after that.

'It all seems a long time ago,' said Elsie, a few days later. 'We live a quiet life now – can't do much else on a pension.' She paused reflectively. 'Your Uncle Ned,' she continued with a note of pride, 'is a reformed character these days, he's out at the moment helping the old people in the flats.'

Hardly had she spoken than there was a scraping noise at the front door as though somebody was trying to open it with a key and not succeeding. Elsie opened the door to find Ned propped against it. His boots clattered on the step. His cap was on sideways, his face was bright red and his blue eyes were bright and unfocussed. 'Gor a double up,' he slurred, 'the two-fifteen and the four-o-clock.' He gave a wide, beaming smile and fell flat on his face in the hallway.

The catch of the day

'The Catch'

Uncle Ned was at a loose end, which was unusual. Normally the only thing loose about him was his trousers. These gave the impression of having been made to measure – for Oliver Hardy. By contrast, his jacket looked more like Stan Laurel's.

Ned had worn thick serge suits since moleskin became unobtainable, a source of regret to a retired riveter. Even on a hot summer day he wore the lot, complete with cap and boots. The only concession was to leave off the muffler so that his sinewy neck stuck out of his collarless shirt in tortoise-like fashion.

It was a hot day and Ned's inclination inevitably led him towards the 'Boilermaker's Arms'. Unfortunately, having made a few unsuccessful bets, he was broke again. Auntie Elsie would not lend him any. She knew too well where it would end up. On pension day she was always the first in the queue at the post office.

It was hot. Elsie was cleaning the house, lunging a brush with powerful thrusts. Ned dodged around, swinging his shins from side to side, holding a newspaper like a shield. It was no use.

'I'm going out,' he declared, with what dignity he could muster. 'Fetch something back for tea then,' ordered Elsie. 'There's nowt 'ere, I mean nothing.' She rarely spoke in dialect since attending the self-improvement classes at the Townswomen's Guild. Only that morning she had been telling Ned about the division of labour in society. He had said he was all in favour of it, the more division the better. Elsie had then explained in a rather superior way that it was something you learned about in Sociology. Ned then began to tell a joke about a man who went into a pub with a crocodile and asked, 'Do you serve Sociologists?' When he was told they did, he said, 'Give me a pint of bitter and give the crocodile a Sociologist'.

Elsie cut him short him short and told him she meant he should do something useful while she cleaned the house. She then referred to Karl Marx, whereupon Ned replied, 'Karl Marx is alright but he's not a patch on Groucho, Harpo, and Chico'. At that point she swept him out of the house.

In the entry he came upon an old woman dressed in rags and carrying a large handbag. Known as Methylated Maggie, she was a local character, often seen going through the dustbins looking for scraps. It was rumoured that she had plenty of money hidden away somewhere. She was said to have been barmy since the war, but harmless enough.

'Leave a few bins for me, luv.' Said Ned in passing, 'I'll need 'em if I can't get something to eat from somewhere.' He made his way down a dusty entry to the bottom road. He passed the 'Boilermaker's Arms' with a visible effort, then, cutting through another narrow passageway near the shipyard, he came to the river. The high tide, glinting dully, rocked a few ramshackle boats moored in a small dock basin, otherwise disused.

'Oy, Ned!,' called a middle-aged man from the deck of one of the boats, 'Nice day for a sail, eh?' 'Ow do, Tony,' replied Ned. 'Can you let me have a couple of fish? – need 'em for tea tonight. It's a matter of life or death.'

Tony laughed in his distinctive yo-yo style. A middle-European, he had lived on his boat for many years, scraping a bare living from fishing. Tony was not his real name; that was unpronounceable. At one time he had sold fish in the 'Boilermaker's Arms' until the landlord became concerned about the reputation of the establishment. Most of the regulars were more concerned about the quality of the beer.

However Tony and his boat were well-known as a source of cheap fish. He seldom had any left on his hands, only the residue which smelt a bit strong. 'Why don't you live in a house?' Ned had asked him, years before. 'Nobody will rent me one,' was the reply. 'Why?' Ned asked. 'Because I am an alien,' Tony answered. Ned was indignant. 'I take a drink meself' he said.

Tony began to untie the mooring ropes and throw them onto the deck in untidy heaps. The boat's engine was thudding slowly, the exhaust giving occasional explosive coughs. 'Just going now for fish,' shouted Tony above the noise. 'You come with me? Catch your own fish, no charge.' Uncle Ned could recognise a bargain. With barely a second to spare he boarded the boat and was soon out in the river.

When the boat was well clear of the shore with its many hazards, Tony stopped the engine and hoisted a small dirty sail on the boat's one stumpy mast. 'Fuel cost money, plenty money,' explained Tony. Ned looked at the sail. It looked like an old tarpaulin. It probably was, he thought. 'Makeshift, like most of Tony's equipment.' The sail did little to propel the boat but the ebb tide took it downriver quite rapidly.

Ned was not really at home on a boat. Like most shipyard workers he had done no seafaring in spite of all the ships he had helped to build. As the river bank receded and open sea appeared ahead, he began to feel distinctly uncomfortable. Even though it was rolling gently in the sunshine, the sea looked somehow menacing. Ned looked at Tony, who fished all year round in all weathers, with new respect.

'Oy! Ned!,' called Tony, 'You look pale - you okay?' When Ned nodded feebly he offered to make him a jam sandwich. 'Plenty jam – taste nice going down, just as nice coming up.' He gave his yo-yo laugh. Ned began to wonder if catching your own fish was such a good idea after all.

Tony threw overboard a rusty anchor attached to a length of rusty chain. He then went into the boat's tiny cabin and brought out two fishing rods. These were held together with plenty of tape. They began to fish.

Ned held his rod dubiously, not sure what to expect, staring meanwhile at a large merchant ship which seemed to be coming uncomfortably close. 'Won't come near us, said Tony, too shallow'. He pointed down, 'twenty feet.' That seemed deep enough for Ned, especially as the shore looked miles away.

It was hot. Ned took off his jacket but Tony kept on his thick jersey, well-smeared with fish residue, that he wore all the time, summer or winter. 'Should be some cod around here,' he muttered, 'they won't bite, too lazy, too much sunshine.' He went into the cabin and made two cups of very strong tea. They smelled of fish, like everything else.

The afternoon wore on. The boat turned with the tide. By now Ned doubted if any fish of any sort existed in the whole estuary. Even Tony was ready to give up. 'Must go back soon. 'Oy yoy', he jerked to his feet as Ned's line began to run out very rapidly. 'Check it, 'ang on'. The two men wrestled with the rod for some time before they could start to reel the fish in.

'Must be the father and mother of all the cod in the sea,' gasped Tony. When the catch came over the side, there were simultaneous yells of fright from Ned and disgust from Tony. A three-foot conger eel was jerking and snapping on the deck.

That was the end of the fishing trip. By the time the eel was subdued the tide was running strongly into the river. Tony had to use some of his precious fuel and grumbled that the trip had been a dead loss. Ned, feeling more cheerful having arrived safely, suggested that it had been a pleasant day out. Tony said that he didn't go to sea for pleasure and those that did would go to hell for a pastime. He gave the eel , wrapped in an old sack, to Ned. 'You caught it. You take it, no charge, next time maybe we catch a bloomin' barracuda.'

The heat of the day was fading as Ned returned home. On his way up the hill he rehearsed what he would say to Elsie. 'I've brought a nice eel, luv. You can stew it and make jellied eel or something. However he could not convince himself that Elsie would be pleased. Experience told him that he would more likely to get the eel wrapped around his neck. With a sigh of defeat he put the creature in the bin and went into the house, empty-handed, to face the music.

He got the full repertoire. All his faults were fully elaborated with numerous examples of his one abiding characteristic, uselessness. Each sentence was like a burst from a machine gun. Ned sat nodding agreement, the only safe strategy.

Auntie Elsie then switched to another familiar theme; her own lost opportunity of a luxurious life if she had only married the pawnbroker's son. She had turned down the catch of a lifetime and ended up with a . . .

The tirade was interrupted by an ear-splitting screech from the entry outside. Methylated Maggie had opened the bin.

The classic

'The Classic'

Uncle Ned awoke feeling hungry. It was a fine Sunday afternoon and Ned had finished his customary nap. And before that he had his customary dinner-time pint at the 'Boilermaker's Arms'.

He felt refreshed and vigorous, ready to eat a panful of stewed oxtail and dumplings before returning to the pub for another skinful of beer. A shadow of regret passed over his rosy countenance; those days had gone. Since Ned had retired from the shipyard his pension scarcely covered what Ned called his 'entrance fee' – the pint he had to make last all night.

This form of torture was occasionally relieved by some benefactor, usually a hopeful amateur writer or a journalist desperate for copy, who was prepared to buy Ned ale in return for tales of 'the good old days'. They always got good value. Ned could describe in detail, trips to the races in horse-drawn wagonettes, the vicious gangs who preyed on racegoers, mass drunken sprees on Saturday nights and barefist fights on the shore fields the next morning.

The tales sounded 'tall' but were understated if anything. Ned clattered down the stairs, braces dangling, and his 'long john' vest buttoned to the neck. 'What's for tea?' he enquired. Auntie Elsie regarded him with a sort of resigned disapproval. She put down the novel she had been reading, a classic love story set in elegant society in which the central character, a poor girl from a shipbuilding town is elevated socially by marrying the son of the shipyard owner.

She looked at Ned and sighed. 'I thought we might have something different today,' she remarked, putting the kettle on the gas cooker. Ned's face dropped. 'Eh?' he exclaimed. Elsie repeated the remark in the piercing tone she used to cope with Ned's deafness, although she was aware that Ned was not as deaf as he made out.

'You've been to that cookery class again, 'ave you?' said Ned, pulling at the laces of his large hobnailed boots. 'You're not going to make that paella stuff again, are you?'

'You always bring that up', said Elsie, crossly. 'That's what I mean,' replied Ned, placing his flat cap on top of his bald head. Elsie fixed him with a look that would have stopped a charging rhinoceros. 'I thought, as it is a pleasant afternoon, we would eat al fresco.'

Ned's jaw dropped. He jerked upright in his chair, shot out of the door, blundered wildly down the backyard and crashed out into the entry. In his haste he tripped over a dustbin frightening a poor elderly person known as Methylated Maggie who had been rummaging in it. She in turn knocked over another bin and the resulting pandemonium caused sash windows to go all down the terrace. Some of the remarks that followed were very provoking, casting doubts upon Ned's intelligence and parentage. He was also advised to take certain actions that would have been virtually impossible to carry out.

Ned was too upset to reply in kind as he might have done on other occasions. He had to drink a pint and a half of best bitter before he began to feel calmer.

'No, no, it's not like that at all,' said Charlie the postman soothingly, as he passed the price of the beer over to 'Arry Wade the landlord. 'Al fresco is from the Italian. It means, 'in the open air.'

'Is that all?' replied Ned, visibly relieved. 'I thought she'd turned cannibal. I mean, who the 'eck is this Al Fresco? I thought she'd gone off her rocker altogether. I blame this 'ere Townswomen's Guild – fills her 'ead with all sorts of nonsense.'

'Having a meal out of doors strikes me as being a civilised idea' said Charlie in his superior way. He had a local reputation as a man of letters. 'Perhaps she was planning a barbecue.'

'A barby what?' asked Ned. 'It's a charcoal fire,' replied Charlie. 'You grill steaks over it.' 'Where'd we get steaks from?' asked Ned scornfully. 'Anyway, I could do better with a rivetter's fire and a pair of long tongs.'

Charlie and 'Arry laughed so uproariously at this that another drinker at the bar was heard to remark, 'this ale is stronger than I thought.'

Ned was not amused and Charlie scenting trouble, motioned with his head towards the door. 'Come and see me new car,' he said. Since buying the car, Charlie had become a car-conversationalist. If anyone said, 'Nice Day,' he would reply, 'A good day for cleaning the car.' Or, if someone asked, 'Have you seen so and so lately?' he would reply something like, 'Yes, he's running this or that make of car; he's having trouble with the shock absorbers'. To the listener, this was tedious to say the least.

Charlie had wanted to own a car since his national service days in the RAF. He cultivated a small moustache, brushed out at the sides, wore a blazer with a RAF badge, and sometimes actually wore a cravat. Even Ned could appreciate that this sort of style would go well with a car, especially a sports car, but was lost on Charlie's post office bike even though he swung it around corners like a Spitfire in combat.

'This is it', said Charlie proudly as he opened the garage door. 'A real classic car.' Ned stared at the car, dubiously. To him it looked very ordinary, not to say dilapidated, with a touch of rust here and there to relieve the dullness of the faded paintwork. 'I'll show you the engine,' said Charlie, enthusiastically tugging at the bonnet catch.

'Hey 'ang on a minute,' said Ned in a tone of slight alarm. 'I've got to get 'ome. Elsie's got a meal ready. Al Fonzo or whatever she calls it. If I stay out any longer it'll be in the bin, and I'm bloomin' famished. I've had nowt to eat since breakfast.'

'I was going to show you me shock absorbers,' said Charlie in a disappointed tone. 'Anyway', he continued, 'hop in and I'll take you for a spin.' 'Oh, I dunno', replied Ned. 'It's not far to walk.' 'I'll run you home', said Charlie breezily, 'It'll save your legs.' Ned got in beside Charlie who was pulling knobs, twisting switches and pushing levers like some demented pilot preparing for take-off.

The engine burst into life, coughing and revving unstably. A sudden jerk threw Ned back into his seat. He heard Charlie shout something about a fierce clutch. before the car, tyres squealing, swung out onto the bottom road, with pedestrians scattering in panic.

Fortunately no other cars, and especially no buses, were about. Ned crouched below the dashboard. Charlie began changing gears like a grand prix driver as the car climbed the hill towards Ned's house. The speed dropped considerably, to Ned's relief, but the engine note increased to a deafening crescendo.

As soon as the car jerked to a stop outside Ned's house, Ned baled out as though leaving a crashing plane. As if to add to the effect, a pall of blue smoke was dispersing gently, all the way up the hill. Ned, landing on the pavement like a parachute artist, drew applause from a few people who were looking at the car in amazement.

The car engine began to splutter and bang. In spite of Charlie pulling knobs and levers in rapid succession, it coughed to a stop. A mist of steam began to fill the car. 'What's wrong with it?' called Ned from the pavement, his voice loud in the sudden silence.

'There's a technical term for what's wrong with it,' replied Charlie, grimly, but I wouldn't use it in polite company.' 'Never mind, eh ?' said Ned cheerfully. 'At least it's all downhill to the garage.' 'Thanks a bunch,' muttered Charlie.

Ned entered the house with a growing feeling of trepidation. What sort of mood would Elsie be in after his hasty exit.

'Where did you get to in such a hurry?' she asked. 'I - er - had to see Charlie,' he lied. 'He brought me home in his car.'

'Oh, aye. Well, there was a right commotion after you left. It sounded like some sort of riot. Then that old woman, the one they call Methylated Maggie, started screaming for help. She said she'd been molested by a man who jumped on her from a great height – said it was Spring-heeled Jack. Do you know anything about it?' 'No, love, not a thing, I'm starving with hunger,' he said, pathetically. He looked at the tiny portion of smoked salmon on a bed of lettuce surrounded by tomatoes and radishes cut into fancy shapes. 'You couldn't do me a stewed oxtail, could you?'

Ned's Cannonball

'The Holiday'

Auntie Elsie had been complaining for some time that she would like a holiday, but it seemed that it could not be afforded out of the pension she and Uncle Ned received. 'Never mind, eh?' said Ned sympathetically, if not exactly tactfully. 'Never mind never mind', she replied irritably. 'You never wanted to go on holiday. It'd be too far away from the 'Boilermaker's Arms' and the betting shop'.

'It's not long since we went to the seaside,' protested Ned. 'Remember we went on the train and the engine broke down?' 'Aye, a steam engine; that shows how long ago it was' replied Elsie. 'We can't afford to go on holiday,' said Ned. 'Tell me something I don't know,' was the acid reply 'If you'd had a bit of ambition we'd have been on a better pension. You could have made something of yourself.' 'You mean like Charlie the postman?' 'Him,' replied Elsie scornfully. 'He's about as much use as a rubber walking stick.'

'That's where you're wrong,' said Ned. 'Charlie helps a lot of people. I'll ask him if he knows of any cheap holidays.' 'Don't bother' replied Elsie. 'I'd just as soon ask for help from Attila the Hun,' 'Don't think I know that feller,' said Ned, putting on his donkey jacket and flat cap to go out.

A few days later, Ned returned from the 'Boilermakers Arms' in jubilant mood. 'Told you Charlie would fix us up. He's got us a week in a self-catering apartment by the sea near Rhyl, and he said he'll take us there in his car.' 'It's a bit early in the year,' said Elsie, dubiously as she watched the wind blow the roofing felt off Ned's backyard shed. 'That's why it's cheap,' said Ned. 'Oh well, I was thinking of going to Spain,' replied Elsie resignedly. 'Maybe next year'. 'Yeah', said Ned, smiling encouragingly, 'Next Year.'

The next weekend Elsie and Ned were ready long before they heard the noise of Charlie's car clattering outside the front door. Elsie had packed food and clothing into an ancient case, the weight of which flattened the car springs. With Charlie grumbling about his shock absorbers and reminding Ned that it was a classic car, they set off.

The journey was uneventful except for some slight confusion as to the correct route. As they approached a roundabout, Charlie asked, 'We turn left here don't we?' 'Right,' said Ned. 'I thought it was left', replied Charlie. 'Right', said Ned. 'You mean right?' asked Charlie. 'No, left' said Ned. 'Make up your mind,' said Charlie irritably, as they circled the roundabout for the second time.

Arriving at last at what was described on a lopsided notice board as a Holiday Park, Charlie seemed to be in a hurry to unload his passengers and go. 'The Warden's house is along the lane' he said, 'just before you get to the chalets.' He drove off in a cloud of blue smoke.

The Warden's house turned out to be a caravan and the self-catering apartment turned out to be an odd sort of chalet. 'It's an old railway carriage,' exclaimed Elsie in disbelief. 'No, it's just got a lot of doors,' said Ned, 'You can have a first class.' 'So can you,' replied Elsie. 'First class clown'. 'It's very well built,' put in the Warden, an elderly man with a strong Welsh accent, 'hardly leaks at all. By the way,' he continued warningly 'be careful if you go swimming. The tide is very strong.'

Elsie looked at him as though he was mad. Between the sand dunes she could see a disused lighthouse and the sea churning along a windswept beach. 'Swimming's the last thing we'd do' she said with a shiver. 'That's what I mean.' said the warden, departing. 'He's a cheerful soul, I don't think,' remarked Elsie, sarcastically.

After a meal concocted out of tins brought from home, Ned went in search of a pub. He returned very late and woke up Elsie by trying to open every door in the 'chalet' except the one that was in use. 'You've got to 'ave a drink on 'oliday,' he slurred. 'So I see' replied Elsie, cutting short his excited account of meeting a friend in the pub who had offered to take him fishing the following day.

The next day Ned went sea fishing, but not before the Warden, who had found out about the proposed trip, came around to warn Ned about the dangers of being cut off or swept away by the tide. As it happened, the type of fishing which Ned and his new-found friend were planning did not involve a boat, as Elsie feared after the trip with Tony, but a long rod casting from the beach. It was relatively safe and totally unsuccessful.

Undeterred by this, the following day the two intrepid fishermen tried stretching a line with hooks attached between two wooden stakes driven into the sand. Ned and his friend spent long thirsty hours watching as the incoming tide covered the line, then, as the water began to ebb away, they saw two or three small fish wriggling on the hooks. Ignoring the warden's warning, they dashed into the surf to get the fish; but the seagulls got there first.

A little later in the week, Ned made enquiries about hiring a boat to go sea fishing but abandoned the idea after the Warden said it would amount to suicide. His confidence as a fisherman was now completely gone and he was reduced to buying fresh fish for Elsie.

Never downcast for long, Ned's optimism returned after he obtained a metal detector from the holiday park shop. He set off along the beach to find treasure. After a cold morning searching the beach, being careful to heed the Warden's advice to watch out for quicksand, Ned found what he thought might be part of a cannonball.

'I hope you're satisfied with messing about on the shore', said Elsie, inspecting the shapeless lump of rusty iron. 'I've had enough of sitting here waiting for you. I want a night out.'

Ned made a token protest about not being able to afford entertainment, and having no transport; but he knew what he had to do. He got the Warden to phone for a taxi and took Elsie to a show in Rhyl.

On the Saturday that the holiday ended the sun came out and the wind dropped for the first time that week. The gently rippling sea looked blue, the sand yellow, and the lighthouse gleaming white.

After a last cup of tea, Elsie and Ned sat on the large, antiquated suitcase waiting for Charlie to pick them up. It was quite pleasant. The Warden came out of his caravan, He seemed unusually cheerful as though glad to be relieved of responsibility. He said they looked sunburned. 'Weatherbeaten,' corrected Elsie. But even she seemed pleased, probably glad to be going home.

'A seaside holiday does you a world of good,' said the Warden, 'Just so long as you keep well away from the sea.' He shook hands with Ned and Elsie. 'Give me a ring if you want to come again,' he said. 'My name's Jones, Davy Jones.'

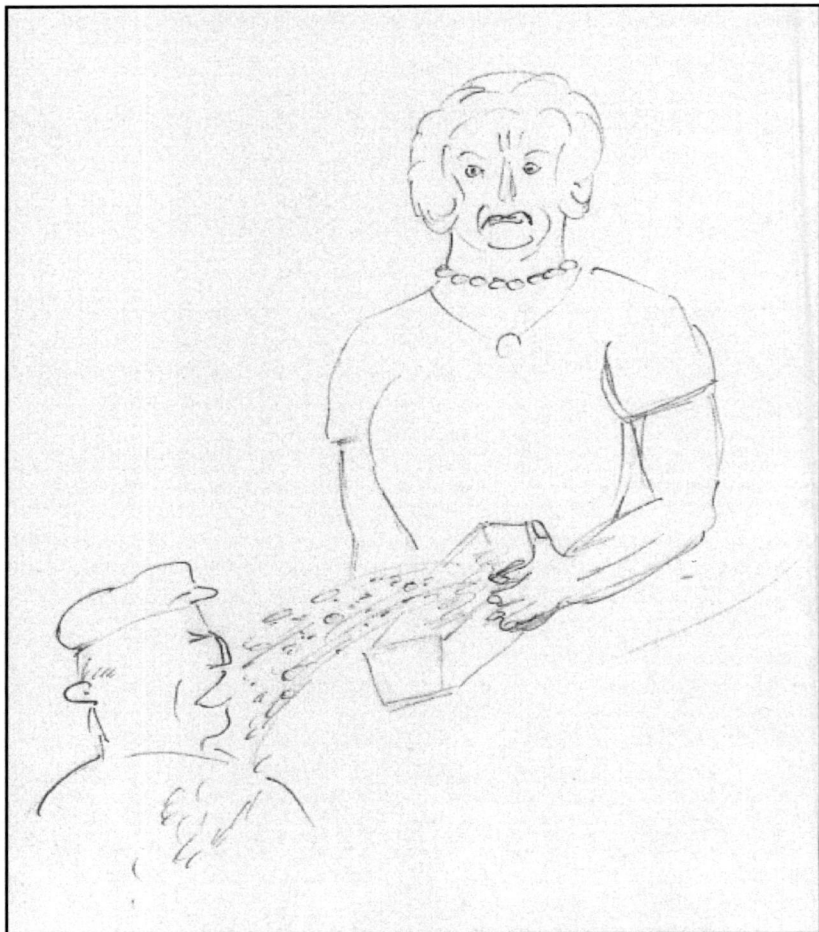

A trying day

'The Handyman'

Uncle Ned was not his usual contented self as he studied the racing page of the morning paper, picking out certainties he had no money to back. He had a feeling that he was in for a trying day. From time to time, his concentration was disturbed by his wife's movements but, with the wisdom of experience, he made no comment.

Auntie Elsie was in a dangerously discontented mood, prowling between the front and the back of their small terraced house. She paused and stared out of the living room at the backyard. 'I'm fed up wi' that,' she said suddenly. Ned jumped several inches, dropping the paper. 'What do you mean, love?' he enquired mildly, picking up the paper and his braces that had slid from his shoulders.

'That, that out there, the backyard,' she snapped, pointing with a hand as large as a man's. 'What's wrong with it?' asked Ned, astonished. 'What's wrong with it?', repeated Elsie. I'll tell you what's wrong with it.' 'I thought you might,' muttered Ned. 'It's old-fashioned, that's what' continued Elsie, ignoring the interruption. 'It's like one of them pictures in the book we studied at the Guild – how the poor lived in Victorian society. I don't want to be reminded of it every time I look out of the window.'

Ned stared at the floor. Then he rose, adjusted his braces, which, incidentally, served no useful purpose as his trousers were held up by a wide, brass-buckled belt, and reached for his stained flat cap.

'Where are you going?' enquired Elsie in a dangerously quiet voice. 'Just for a walk, love, a bit of fresh air, like.' 'Well think on. I want something done about that backyard.' 'Like what?' asked Ned. 'A conservatory,' she replied. 'I don't want one of them - I've told you before - I always vote Labour' said Ned, accelerating his steps as he caught sight of Elsie's expression.

Ten minutes later Ned was at the bar of the 'Boilermaker's Arms' a half-pint of mild in his hand and a long-suffering expression on his weatherbeaten face. 'We were content until she started going to them classes and getting ideas above her station' he said to his pal Charlie 'she went in for this continental cooking. Somebody called Gordon Blue was teaching 'em. I had to buy her a pressure cooker.'

'Yeah, yeah', I know the score.' He began to down his second pint of bitter. 'So do I', said Ned, 'and its one-nil to 'er. 'Anyway' he continued 'What do you know about it? you're still single.' 'I don't need to jump in the fire to know it's 'ot.' Faced with this unanswerable logic, Ned fell silent.

The landlord, 'Arry Wade, leaned over the bar. 'We 'ad one of them pressure cookers –it exploded.' He paused to let the information sink in. 'Scouse was plastered all over the wall when I came in from school. Where's Ma? I said', and Dad said 'She's in 'ospital.' So I said 'What are we going to do? and he said 'I'll open a tin of corned beef. He was an 'ard beggar, was me Dad.'

'He needed to be' said Ned. 'Some hard characters used to come in 'ere in them days. They used to spend some money, not like now. They'd all come in straight from work smelling of rust and sweat, clamouring to get served.'

'We served 'em all right. If Churchill had come in he'd have got two pints straight away.' Charlie, being somewhat younger than the other two, became impatient with their reminiscing. He drained his glass, muttered, 'Work to do', and left. Ned gazed sorrowfully at his empty glass. 'You know, 'Arry,' he said. 'I'm thinking of going back to work.' 'Where?' asked 'Arry. 'The shipyard's closed.' 'Well – er - Charlie said he could get me a job as a handyman at Fred's Tool Hire. He promised to put a word in for me.'

'Don't take too much notice of him,' advised 'Arry. 'Did you hear about his driving test? It seems the Post Office wanted him to transfer off the bike onto a van, so they sent him on a crash course.' 'Did he pass?' 'No, he crashed.'

Ned pondered this information in the light of the fact that Charlie the postman actually owned a car. He decided that 'Arry must be mistaken.' 'I'll give it a try anyway.' He said. 'Don't say I didn't warn you,' replied 'Arry, gazing round the bar, now empty except for Ned.

Fred's Tool Hire occupied part of a small, long-disused quarry on the opposite side of the road to the pub. It had formerly been a scrap woodyard owned by an old man who claimed to have sparred with Jack Johnson. The old man had lived to be ninety-five and, according to Charlie, had come from a long-lived family Even his dog lived to be fifteen.

More recently the yard had become an enclosure of lock-up garages and small businesses such as Fred's Tool Hire. 'Charlie sent you, did he?' asked Fred, a middle aged man in greasy overalls who spent much of his time wishing he had spent his redundancy money to start some other kind of business, something easier and more secure, like rent-collecting on the Dock Road Estate. 'That's right,' said Ned. 'He said he was your best customer.'

Fred put down a bundle of tangled electric flex. The temporary floodlights to which it was attached appeared to have been used for target practice. 'He uses plenty of me tools,' agreed Fred, 'jacks, stands, spanners – you name it. Trouble is –he pays nowt.'

'I'm looking for work,' said Ned. 'I'm fed up with being retired; there's no money in it.' Fred looked thoughtful. 'The shipyard's closed' he said. 'I know that,' replied Ned irritably. 'I can do other things beside bash rivets. I can do, well, all sorts of things. I can make anything, except money.' He concluded lamely.

'I tell you what,' said Fred,' you could go and collect some of me equipment. Start with that take-away chip shop in Unity Street and get me carpet shampoo cleaner back. They had an accident; pressure cooker exploded.' 'Unity Street!' exclaimed Ned. 'I've not been down there for years. It used to be a right tough area. On a Saturday night even the police needed police protection.'

Fred was not listening. He was shaking his head at the state of the lamps. 'New a month ago,' he muttered. 'I should have gone into the entertainment business as a contortionist.' 'Don't you mean a snake charmer?' suggested Ned, looking at the cable. Turning suddenly, as if he had just noticed Ned's presence, Fred said in a business-like way, 'Get on with it. Make sure you get the cleaner back, and the payment for the hire of it.'

Unity Street looked peaceful enough in the afternoon sunshine. Most of the notorious slum housing behind the shops had been demolished. The chip shop, which was next to the public toilets, now had a large coloured sign, 'Silver Spray Take-away. Full Oriental Menu.'

The proprietor, clad in a singlet and denims was stirring the boiling vats. 'Open ten minute,' he called cheerfully. Sounds of chopping came from the kitchen behind him. 'You like order?.' 'I'm from Fred's Tool Hire' said Ned. The proprietor's face fell. 'Ah, yes. We had accident.' 'A pressure cooker, wasn't it?' said Ned. 'No, no. It was me wok.' 'Yer what, wack?'

'Me wok,' said the proprietor, picking up a huge iron pan. 'Vely good for sorting out tlouble-makers.' 'You hit 'em with that?' asked Ned, incredulously. 'Yah. Works evely time. Unfortunately, I forgot it was full of bean shoots.'

Ned decided to get down to business. 'I'll take the machine, if you've finished with it.' 'No ploblem,' said the proprietor, reaching under the counter and handing over a large cleaning machine. 'What about the hire payment?' asked Ned, one eye on the wok and ready to make a swift departure.

The man's smile disappeared. He hit the till with what looked like a karate chop and the ancient machine crashed open with a ringing noise. 'Empty, no customers, no money. Later, plenty customers, plenty money.' 'Sounds reasonable to me', said Ned, shouldering the cleaning machine.

'Wait,' said the man, 'One minute please'. He turned towards the kitchen and shouted in a high-pitched voice. The noise of chopping increased and in a short time a carrier bag was handed out. 'Here you are,' said the man, smiling broadly. Number four special banquet for two, with chips and flied lice. On the house.'

By the time Ned arrived back at Fred's Tool Hire, the machine was cutting into his shoulder and he was sweating. 'Did you get the hire money?' asked Fred eagerly. 'Not exactly' replied Ned. 'You'll have to get that yourself. He's got a wok. But I've got your machine back. That should be worth a pint or two.' 'Aye said Fred without enthusiasm, 'I'll see you right next time I'm in the 'Boilermaker's Arms'. 'You know,' he continued, examining the machine which was clogged with what looked like bean shoots, 'I shouldn't be in this business at all. I could have been a neurological surgeon, but I didn't have the brains.'

Remembering that Fred seldom visited the pub, and when he did he was not renowned for generosity, Ned decided to waste no more of his time. Trudging homewards, he reflected that he had got something for his efforts, a free meal for two. Things could have been worse.

When Ned arrived home the dining table was laid and a steamy smell was coming from the kitchen. It reminded him of wash days in years gone by. 'I got a take away, love' he announced. 'Take away', repeated Elsie, incredulously. 'You've never as much as brought a bag of chips home before now. Anyway, I've made a meal, something special, a cannelloni.' Uncle Ned looked less than enthusiastic. 'Aw, eh, love,' he complained. 'You know I don't like canned food.'

There followed a sudden shout of alarm, a swift clatter of hobnailed boots in the backyard, and Ned was out in the back entry, spattered and festooned with the number four banquet.

It had been a trying day.

There was an almighty splash

'Racecourse Revisited'

In spite of his encyclopaedic knowledge of horse racing, Uncle Ned had been to very few actual race meetings, especially in recent years, since his retirement. His reputation as an expert had been built up over many years in the 'Boilermaker's Arms' and on 'The Paddock', a rough grassy area near to the allotments where gamblers studied form and placed their bets through the services of runners, some of whom had of pocketing the stake money, especially if the horse had no chance. Of course, if the horse did win, then the runner had to run as never before, as fast and as far away as possible.

The establishment of betting shops, unknown in Ned's younger days, put a stop to that practice. The betting shops are not known for diddling their clients, perhaps in some measure because they cannot run away.

One fine day in spring, Ned had been standing at the bar of the 'Boilermaker's Arms' telling tales of his visits to local racecourses and of his successes in placing bets. Two young men, well-dressed strangers to the pub, who were listening to Ned's boasting, were not very impressed. It was a fairly obvious question, why was Ned propping up the bar of a small, street-corner pub, dressed in a flat cap, donkey jacket, stained working trousers and heavy boots, if he could pick winners so successfully?

Far from buying Ned a pint, as he had hoped, the two young men seemed bored and declared betting to be a mug's game, 'Only fit for them old blokes in the park.' They ordered bottles of top-price lager and, to Ned's astonishment, drank it straight from the bottle.

After the young men had left, Ned sat in a depressed mood. The young men seemed to have plenty of money to spend and all day to do it. What, he wondered were designer jeans? and why did those thick-soled plimsolls they call trainers cost more than Ned had been accustomed to pay for a whole outfit of clothing?

Charlie the postman arrived for his customary 'liquid lunch'. He was sweating from pedalling his heavy post office bike up steep hills. 'Talk about occupational fitness,' he muttered, 'much more of this and I'll be ready for the Mr Universe contest.' 'Legs only,' commented Ned. ''Ave a pint,' said Charlie, ignoring the veiled insult.

'Very civil of yer,' replied Ned, swiftly sinking the half pint he had been sipping for the last hour. He told Charlie about his encounter with the two young men. 'Well, I can see their point of view,' said Charlie, 'What can they know about going to races in charabangs and all that? It's a different world.' 'You can say that again,' said Charlie.

'It's a ....Oh, never mind. Tell you what, there's racing at Chester next week.' 'I know that,' said Ned, 'fat chance of me being there.' 'Why not?' asked Charlie, 'I'll take you there in me car, Okay?'

After Charlie left, Ned finished his pint in more cheerful mood. A trip to the races had always been the highlight of his year, especially in the days when he had plenty of money to spend, or waste as Auntie Elsie would describe it. After his retirement he had resigned himself to seeing racing on the betting shop television.

The day of the races dawned clear, promising a fine day. Ned awoke from a dream in which he had been reliving his one and only boyhood holiday; a working holiday on a farm. Every morning at daybreak the farmer's dilapidated tractor had driven up to the hut where the boys slept. Any boy not wakened by the clattering of the vehicle would be roused by the farmer's boot.

Ned rose in a panic, grabbing for his clothes until he realised that the racket was not the long-ago tractor, but Charlie's car. Elsie jerked up right in bed, her curlers springing off her head. 'Gas,' she yelled in terror. 'Where's me mask?' She then sank back in embarrassed confusion. 'Thought it was one of them rattle things they 'ad in the war.'

She jumped again as a siren-like noise sounded. It was Charlie's hooter. 'Old yer bloomin' 'orses will yer,' shouted Ned from the bedroom window. 'Urry up', replied Charlie over the noise of the engine. 'It'll overheat in a minute.' 'Can't yer switch it off?' yelled Ned. 'No, it mightn't start again,' bellowed Charlie.

A cloud of steam had begun to envelope the car. Neighbours began to open windows and enquire, none too politely, what all the noise was about. Ned replied, even less politely with advice that would have been painful, if not impossible for them to take. In the midst of all the confusion, Ned was propelled by Elsie out of the front door and into the car. He was wearing his one and only suit at Elsie's insistence. She said the cream of the county would be present at the races and he must be properly dressed.

They set off for Chester to mix with the cream of the county. Charlie, complaining about the delay, said, 'You can't hurry these classic cars you know.' The temperature gauge was already in the red. 'If it gets any 'otter, we'll be boiled,' replied Ned, wiping his bald head with large handkerchief.

Finally, with the engine rattle getting harsher by the minute, they pulled into a car park. 'This is it', said Charlie. 'Ere, wait a minute,' said Ned. 'This isn't the bloomin' racecourse. This is the zoo.' 'This is the park and ride,' explained Charlie. 'We'd never get a parking place in the City on race day.'

'What will they think of next?' said Ned.

Arriving at the racecourse they found it thronged with people. A few reserved parking spaces were already occupied by Rolls-Royces and other prestigious vehicles. Only one space remained and, as they watched a very strange car drove into it. Charlie gaped at the tiny old-fashioned body perched on top of enormous wheels. The car was painted matt black except what looked like tongues of fire around the base. 'It's a customised Popular, he said admiringly.' Ned was looking at the occupants. 'It's them lads who were in the pub,' he said in amazement.

'The stewards will soon shift them,' said Charlie. But the official who hurried over merely opened the door and saluted. 'Crikey!' exclaimed Charlie. Later, after the race meeting started, Ned and Charlie encountered the two lads again. They were running a bookmaker's stand. A board above their heads read, 'Joe Horswill, the Old Firm.'

Ned, who was more knowledgeable on such matters, nudged Charlie. 'That's one of the biggest bookmaking firms in the north of England. They run the betting shop I go to.' He went over to the stand and placed a bet. The young man, though busy, recognised him. 'Come to try your luck, granddad?' 'I thought you said betting's a mug's game?' replied Ned, 'So I did,' he said. 'Well, you seem to be doing alright. Do you work for Joe Horswill?' 'No, he works for us. We took him over. Now he looks after the shops and we do the on-course work.' 'Blimey!' exclaimed Ned. There didn't seem to be much more he could say.

To Ned's further amazement, his horse won, and so did the next, and the next. All in all Ned took a sizeable sum of money off Joe Horswill, the old firm. The two lads took it philosophically. 'You'll lose it all in the betting shop or at the next race meeting.' This rather patronising statement made Ned determined not to lose his winnings to the bookies. He did, however, spend a fair amount of it celebrating his win at the bar, with the result that he was the worse for wear by the end of the meeting. He managed to lurch on rubber legs as far as the gate, but it was obvious that he could not walk as far as the park and ride bus.

'What the 'eck are we going to do now? said Charlie.'It's all your fault,' slurred Ned, 'rushin' me out of the house this morning. I'ad no time for me breakfast.' Charlie noticed the two young men getting into their car. 'Hey, lads, I mean gents could you give us a lift to the park and ride? My friend's a bit under the weather.'

The lads took a look at Ned who was doing a sort of walking on the spot. 'Ratted,' one of them said. 'As a newt,' said the other. 'What can I do with him?' asked Charlie in desperation. 'We can't take you,' said one of the lads. 'We're going to a reception with the horse trainers. I'll tell you what, our cruiser's just around the corner, on the canal. Put him in it to sleep it off. You can't miss it. It's called 'The Hot Favourite'. He put the car in gear and drove off with a bellow of noise from the exhaust.

Fortunately the canal was not far away and the cruiser was

a conspicuous mound of white fibreglass among the dark-coloured traditional boats. Charlie, sweating from supporting Ned, began to unfasten the boat's cover. Ned, left unattended for a moment, fell into the canal. There was an almighty splash, then a shout from Ned, 'Help, I can't swim.' A crowd gathered, some shouting, 'Stand up it's only three feet deep.' But Ned, plunging about like a hippopotamus, was unable to stand. Somebody threw a lifebelt which Ned grasped and he was pulled up onto the towpath where he promptly collapsed in a heap.

An ambulance was called which took Ned to the hospital where he was checked for damage which was surprisingly slight. He was not even drunk any more. The cold water immersion had sobered him. His clothes had been hung in the drying room next to a powerful heater.

After a couple of hours, Ned was discharged. The taxi driver who took Ned and Charlie to the park and ride looked dubiously at the banknote offered by Ned. It looked like a crisp lettuce leaf. When Ned finally arrived home, Auntie Elsie was in bed. She did not seem to be surprised that he had stayed out well past midnight, but knowing he had been to a race meeting, she was surprised that he had not stayed out all night.

Almost speechless at his appearance, all she could say was, 'What happened to your suit?' 'It got wet,' replied Ned, 'it shrunk.' He tried to pull down the sleeves which were halfway up his arms. 'Got wet? How?' asked Elsie. 'Don't ask,' replied Ned wearily. 'Oh well,' said Elsie, 'I always thought you should be in a straight-jacket.'

"Abyssinia"

'Uncle Ned goes back to School'

Uncle Ned sat at the breakfast table. His collarless shirt was unbuttoned showing his long-john vest; his braces hung down over his thick serge trousers. He lifted his glass of orange juice and drained it at a gulp. Auntie Elsie regarded him with distaste.

'When are you going to find something useful to do?' she asked. 'I've been looking,' Ned replied. 'Anyway', he continued defensively, 'I couldn't do much work on this sort of breakfast. Why can't I 'ave bacon and sausage and fried bread?' 'The lady at the Townswomen's Guild said we all need a balanced diet with plenty of calcium, iron and potassium,' replied Elsie. 'I saw enough iron when I used to work in the shipyard,' said Ned, 'and as for the other stuff - I'll go and buy you a chemistry set.'

'Don't get sarcastic with me,' warned Elsie, 'it's for your own good, though why I bother I don't know. I could have married the pawnbroker's son and had a life of comfort instead of scraping and scratching while you spend all your wages in the pub and the betting shop.' 'Aw, put another record on,' muttered Ned wearily. 'What did you say?' snapped Elsie. 'Nowt love,' he replied mildly. 'Can I 'ave a cup of tea? That orange juice gives me wind.' 'You can go and earn some money instead of spending it.'

'Aw, eh, love,' complained Ned, 'I 'aven't finished this muesli stuff yet. Tell the truth I don't much like it. I'd sooner 'ave a bowl of porridge with plenty of milk.' 'Get out,' snapped Elsie. 'Yes, love, just

59

going,' said Ned, hastily grabbing his flat cap and not even bothering to lace up his hobnailed boots.

Out in the entry he placed his foot on a bin, tied his bootlaces and considered his options. For a retired riveter, well on in his sixties, paid work of any sort was hard to come by. He removed his cap and scratched his bald head. The entry was deserted except for himself and an old homeless woman known as 'Methylated Maggie' who was rummaging in the bins. She scuttled away nervously as Ned approached. 'Where are they?' she croaked.' 'Who?' asked Ned. 'Them boys what make fun of me,' 'They'll all be at school,' replied Ned. 'best place for 'em if you ask me.'

Ned walked on, leaving the old woman to her scavenging. She was a well-known local character, barmy since the war but quite harmless. The same gang of lads who were making her life even more miserable were causing mayhem around the area, particularly at the old people's flats where Charlie the postman acted as unofficial minder and helper. He had mentioned in the pub that he was fed up with them and offered his solution - a good thrashing. A pity the shipyard was closed, thought Ned, a few weeks as a riveter's apprentice would do 'em some good.

Wandering aimlessly on, Ned came to the school. The old red brick building at the front was the same elementary school that Ned had attended. After the war new buildings had been added and the school became a secondary modern. Now it was a comprehensive. As it was mid-morning, too early to go for a drink, Ned decided to ask if there was a chance of any casual work.

By a stroke of good fortune the Caretaker came to the gate. He was a thin, stooping character in a scruffy anorak. Ned knew him slightly and remembered him from thirty years before. Then he had been dressed in a smart uniform, almost like a soldier or a policeman.

'Things 'ave changed a bit,' observed Ned, nodding a greeting to the man. 'Aye, you could say that,' agreed the Caretaker gloomily. 'Don't you wear your peaked cap?' asked Ned. 'I've been denoted,' 'Pardon,' said Ned. 'Denoted, I used to be the Janitor, now I'm just the Caretaker.'

'Oh, you mean demoted,' said Ned. He was having difficulty

understanding the Caretaker's speech. The man's false teeth clattered up and down as if they had a life of their own. 'They used to do things properly in the old days,' complained the Caretaker. 'You knew where you were. Now they do everything with a blooming commuter. The school's got too big-too many kids. I blame this 'ere copulation explosion.'

'Don't you mean?' began Ned. 'Eh?' said the man. 'Nothing,' replied Ned, 'You got it right the first time.' 'Well,' said the Caretaker, 'I got work to do.' He moved away, 'Abyssinia.' Ned, puzzled by the last word, nearly lost his chance. ''Ang on a minute,' he called, 'I'm looking for work.'

'Come on then,' said the Caretaker, surprisingly promptly. Ned followed him to a small shed that was obviously his den. Nearby was a temporary classroom. It looked dilapidated and strange sounds were being emitted.

'That's the music class,' explained the Caretaker. 'They're learning the bassoon.' 'What, teaching a monkey?' asked Ned, perplexed. Ignoring this, the Caretaker pointed to a stack of cardboard boxes piled up outside of the classroom. 'These are the new music textbooks, 'First steps on the violin'. 'Didn't know you stepped on 'em' said Ned. 'Mind you, considerin' the noise they make, it might be an improvement.'

'Come on,' said the Caretaker impatiently, 'we got to get them books indoors in case it rains.' By the time Ned had carried the boxes into the stock room, while the Caretaker merely told him where to stack them, he was sweating. 'I could do with a drink,' he said. 'I'll make you a cup of tea if you like,' suggested the Caretaker.

'Thanks,' replied Ned, 'but I'd sooner have a pint. Just give me me pay for half a morning's work and I'll be off.' 'Pay? Who said anything about pay? I can't pay you. I'm not cauterised' replied the Caretaker. 'You'll be worse than cauterised if you get me on a mug's game like that again' said Ned angrily.

'Eh what?' replied the Caretaker in a flustered manner. Ned looked him straight in the eye. 'I've only one thing to say to you.' 'Oh aye, what's that?

'Abyssinia.'

Elsie reads a story

'The Function'

Uncle Ned had never been interested in self-improvement for its own sake. He only learned what he thought was necessary, for instance, he could work out the odds on any bet faster than a bookmaker's clerk. And he could tell the lucky winners how much they should receive, which occasionally saved them from being short changed; and gained Ned the price of a pint. He was a true pragmatist.

Auntie Elsie was, by contrast, a dedicated seeker of knowledge. Like Ned she had attended the local elementary school, but she had been in the top class while Ned had been in a notorious 'sin bin' where teachers feared to tread, except the Headmaster, who had to retire early due to arthritis in his right arm probably caused by over-exertion with the cane.

Elsie's main source of enlightenment was the Townswomen's Guild where she learned social and cultural skills. Although she regarded Ned as uncouth, and to be fair to her, he was uncouth, she tried periodically to improve him. One such occasion was the Guild open social evening when members entertained their guests. 'It'll do you good to come,' said Elsie, make a change from the pub, and it won't cost you owt, I mean anything, and you'll get tea and biscuits. 'What, no beer?' enquired Ned. 'I'll see if they've got champagne' replied Elsie, sarcastically'. 'I don't like that. It gives me wind,' said Ned.

Ten minutes later Ned was in the 'Boilermaker's Arms' having been ejected from home by an irate Elsie. 'I suppose I'll 'ave to go,' moaned Ned to his crony, Charlie. 'Don't reckon you've got much option if Elsie's doing a turn,' said Charlie. 'Is she in a sketch or something?' 'Worse than that,' replied Ned. 'She's reading a poem she wrote herself.'

'Your only chance to get out of it is to say you've got nothing to wear,' said Charlie. 'Aye, that's it.' said Ned. 'Me only suit was ruined after I fell in the canal.' 'You can borrow my blazer if you like,' offered Charlie. 'Whose side are you on?' replied Ned. 'Anyway, it's got a big RAF badge on it. I did me war service in the shipyard. The only flying I did was when I fell off the scaffolding.'

When Ned arrived home, slightly unsteady, his flat cap askew, his idea for getting out of it was promptly squashed by Elsie. 'We'll go to the gents outfitters and get you a suit.' 'Who's going to pay for it?' said Ned. 'Me I suppose. I'd rather do without a new dress than have you sitting there like a waxwork of Crippen.'

A few days later Ned and Elsie entered the portals of what had been a high class tailoring establishment, now a little blighted like most of the town centre. The shop had a fine neo-classical façade, a little defaced by posters. Some people called the shop the 'acropolis', others, more unkindly, the 'acrapolis'.

The interior of the shop was very dark, which may have caused Ned to try to ascend the down escalator. In a flurry of arms and clattering boots, he grasped the arm of a large woman on the adjacent up elevator. Her screams brought the security guard who was dressed like a comic opera general, his cap obscuring most of his vision. Elsie hustled Ned away before the guard arrived. The guard was last seen retreating to his cubby hole, capless and pursued by the large woman.

In the suit department, Elsie examined most of the stock before making a choice. 'Go and try it on.' She said. 'Eh?' replied Ned, wondering if he was expected to change there and then. An elderly assistant directed Ned to a fitting room that he unlocked with a plastic card. 'It's for security' he explained, 'we call it a swipe card.' 'You mean in case the stuff gets swiped?' said Ned. 'Precisely, sir,' replied the man, with a blank look.

On the evening of the function, Ned looked quite presentable, not at all like Crippen, more like Lenin. He sat at the back while Elsie sat at the front, ready to recite and looking distinctly nervous. The Chairwoman opened the proceedings by introducing the President, an older and even larger lady. She explained that the function was to display the more cultural side of the Guild's activities as well as the social and charitable work carried out by dedicated members.

Ned's neighbour was frantically adjusting a hearing aid. 'Did she say desiccated?' he asked Ned. 'Dunno,' replied Ned who was not really listening. The Chairwoman continued by saying that the guest speaker was unable to be present to launch his latest book entitled 'Writing for Riches', as he has been summoned for tax evasion. 'Consequently,' she continued, 'we have what our Sociology students would call a dysfunction.' 'What's that?' asked the man with the hearing aid. 'She means he had to go to another function, so he couldn't come to Dis Function.' replied Ned.

'However,' continued the Chairwoman, 'we have a wealth of talent here among our own members who will I am sure, rise to the occasion and treat us to a little more of their work than was planned originally.' Elsie went a whiter shade of pale. 'Me missus won't like that,' confided Ned. 'She's only got one poem.' 'Eh?' said his neighbour. 'The sooner this is over and we can get out for a drink the better,' said Ned. 'Bitter did you say, mine's a pint,' said the man. 'You ain't as deaf as you make out,' observed Ned.

There followed a cello recital the deep droning toes of which increased the drowsiness that had already afflicted half of the audience. A talk on countryside conservation that seemed to have been stretched to suit the occasion did little to stimulate the meeting, nor did a display of abstract paintings, some of which fell on the front row. Then it was time for Elsie's recitation. After much clearing of the throat, Elsie began reciting her poem. It was a lament about a young girl who broke off her engagement to a pawnbroker's son and instead married a riveter, a decision she afterwards regretted. She sat down to polite applause. 'She mixed up the last two lines' said Ned. 'What's the odds?' said the man with the hearing aid.'

'And now,' cried the Chairwoman, as though introducing a circus act, 'following that very interesting poem with a surprise ending, Elsie will read a story from an anthology entitled "Kitchenwriter wants you," which as you know enables many of our writing group to see themselves in print, provided they buy the book of course, ha ha ha. They'll publish anything, ha ha, I mean, ahem, anything of merit. I've a few copies left at £9.99 each.'

Elsie cleared her throat vigorously and began again. 'The story I have chosen is called "A Man of Many Parts." Ned settled back in his chair. His companion made frantic adjustments to his hearing aid. The story turned out to be about a retired shipyard worker who kept getting into bizarre difficulties due to his own ineptitude.

Ned laughed raucously. 'I dunno where these writers get their ideas from. I mean, nobody 'd be that stupid.' 'Aye, maybe,' said the other man doubtfully, looking at Ned. 'Yeah, well, as I said,' continued Ned, 'It's nowt to do with me. I'll tell you what though. When I can get a word with Elsie, I'll ask her who wrote it.'

Maggie's kitchen

'The Detectives'

Uncle Ned sipped his lunchtime pint of bitter and reflected that retirement was, as he put it, not all that it was cracked up to be. The 'Boilermakers Arms' was almost empty, much to the concern of the landlord, 'Arry Wade, who was wiping the bar top and washing what few glasses that had been used. 'Good ale, isn't it?' he asked in rather puzzled tones. Ignoring Ned's offer to assist with the testing, he continued, 'It's always been good ale here – no chemicals.' 'Elsie keeps going on about chemicals in food,' said Ned, 'When I was a lad we didn't bother about chemicals; remember the old bakery down by the railway? No chemicals in their bread, eh?' 'No,' replied 'Arry, 'just the odd cockroach.'

The discussion was interrupted by the entrance of Charlie the postman. 'What are you doing here at dinner time?' asked Ned, 'no letters to deliver?' 'Never mind that,' replied Charlie in a flustered manner, 'there's been a burglary at the old peoples' flats. Can you give me a hand?' 'How about a drop of fortification first,' suggested Ned, never one to miss an opportunity. 'Okay, just a swift half.' 'Good 'ealth', said Ned, draining his glass in one long swallow.

A few minutes later they were walking briskly along the main road, Charlie pushing his red post office bike and Ned, who had, not very politely, declined a ride on the crossbar, clattering alongside in his hobnailed boots. They passed a dismal-looking park where old men sat studying the racing pages. A little further on stood a new block of flats where several senior citizens had found refuge from the cold and loneliness. Some were well-known characters such as Mr Denham, the old soldier, and Methylated Maggie who had been rescued from sleeping rough, mainly through the efforts of Charlie the postman. It was her flat that had been burgled.

Arriving at the flats, Charlie and Ned climbed the stairs to the first landing and knocked at Maggie's door. While waiting they noticed that graffiti had appeared on the newly-painted walls, A sprayed D.H. defaced the gable end. 'That's Darren Head's handiwork', said Charlie, 'he's one of the worst trouble-makers around here. The police call him 'Richard'.

A door opened further down the landing and a neatly dressed elderly man emerged. His white moustache jutted angrily, 'I believe there's been a break-in.' he said in a sharp, authoritative manner. 'This sort of thing needs stamping on straight away, teach them a lesson. A course of recruit training would do them a world of good.' 'Take it easy, Mr Denham,' said Charlie, 'the war's over. Has anyone sent for the police?' 'I believe someone has,' Mr Denham replied, 'but all they seem to do is issue warnings.'

The door in front of them opened suddenly. 'Blimey! exclaimed Charlie, 'What a mess'. 'They never got in 'ere.' said Maggie,' They only got as far as the kitchen. They pinched some of me food. I 'ope it choked 'em'. 'Probably did,' muttered Charlie under his breath. 'Come and look at me kitchen,' invited Maggie. 'No thanks,' said Charlie, 'we'll wait until the police get here.'

'Somebody mention me? ' A veteran police constable stepped through the doorway. He seemed to fill the room. 'PC Stoat at your service. I'm a bit out of breath from climbing the stairs. A cup of tea wouldn't go amiss'.

'I can give you a drop of wine,' offered Maggie. 'Not when I'm on duty, thank you, Madam,' replied the policeman, noticing Charlie's vigorous head shake. He pulled out a portable radio and spoke into it. He received a buzzing crackling reply that sounded like a series of abbreviations, one of which was CID. 'I dunno what the world's coming to,' he said, 'They said it's a job for the CID. The chief himself is coming. They must be short of work. Jack Corncrake hasn't been out of the office for years. He used to be with the Met, they called him Corncrake of the Yard.'

Footsteps sounded on the landing and a young-looking man entered. He was dressed in an expensive-looking leather jacket, jeans and shoes with gold chains across the front. 'You can go now, constable. CID is here' he said. 'Don't you call me constable,' said the uniformed man, 'you're only a con yourself.'

As he spoke another, older man arrived, gasping from climbing the stairs. He wore a dark suit, shiny with age and a battered trilby hat. He was very tall, but gaunt, with the appearance of an elderly ex-boxer. 'Chief Inspector Corncrake,' he said, pushing past the bewildered Maggie. 'Done a thorough job here,' he said. 'It's in the kitchen' said PC Stoat. 'Haven't you got a school crossing to supervise?' asked the young detective. 'All right Constable' said the Chief Inspector. 'Leave this to us.' 'You're welcome to it....Sir,' said PC Stoat, departing with an air of restrained anger.

The two CID men entered the kitchen. The Chief Inspector began pacing about. 'Get on the radio,' he snapped. 'Get the fingerprint squad, get the forensics, get the . . .' 'Hang on a minute,' interrupted the assistant, 'the radio's in the car.' 'Well, gerron with it!' shouted the Chief.

Charlie looked at Ned. 'We may as well go. They don't seem to want to talk to us.' They descended the stairs, collected the post office bike that, to Charlie's relief, was still where he had left it, and went out into the road. They passed the police car in which the detective constable was gabbling into the radio, oblivious to the young children swinging from the wing mirrors.

Coming from the direction of the park was the community policeman, PC Stoat. He was gripping the denim jacket of a skinny youth who was mouthing some very rude words. 'That was quick,' said Charlie. 'How do you know he did it? I mean, you weren't in the kitchen more than a minute.' 'We all know Richard's tricks,' replied the policeman, while the youth objected in the most obscene terms to being called Richard. 'It doesn't need a DCI to solve this case,' said PC Stoat who seemed to have recovered his sense of humour. In fact he was positively beaming. 'This 'ere genius had only gone and sprayed DH right across the kitchen wall.'

The end of the rock concert

'The Easter Turkey'

The landlord of the 'Boilermakers Arms', young 'Arry Wade was inclined to pessimism, even on a bright spring day with Easter just around the corner. 'I don't see much chance of trade picking up,' he said, 'I may as well retire, same as you.' 'Aw, don't do that,' objected Ned. 'This ale's the best in town.' 'It should be,' grumbled 'Arry, 'I sell so little it matures in the barrel.' 'Mind you,' put in Ned, tactlessly, 'It's cheaper at the Legion.' 'Why don't you go there?' replied 'Arry. 'I'm loyal ain't I?' said Ned. He didn't mention that the only reason he hadn't defected to the Legion was that he had never been in uniform.

A gloomy silence fell. 'Arry and Ned stood like wax figures in some heritage park mock-up of an old- time back street pub. Suddenly the door opened, letting in a shaft of sunlight. Charlie the postman, sweating in the midday heat, made straight for the bar. 'Pint of bitter,' he croaked. Noticing Ned's expression of dog-like expectancy, he added, 'make it two.'

'What are you sweating for?' asked Ned, ungratefully. 'All you do is ride a bike.' 'Up and down hills all day'. replied Charlie, 'I've got the worst round in town.' 'Better than bashing rivets,' said Ned. 'Better than trying to make a living out of a pub nobody comes to,' put in 'Arry.

'You want to make it more attractive,' suggested Charlie, 'like that new theme pub down by the river. It's called 'The Liberty Boat,' they got a beer garden with benches out of some old church, and fishing nets 'anging on the wall an' old pictures'. 'Where'd I put a beer garden?'

interrupted 'Arry, 'in the back yard? It's got a fine view of the railway.' 'You could turn it into a Victorian pub.' Suggested Ned, 'put gaslights in.' 'It's only a few years since I 'ad the gaslights taken out.' replied 'Arry.

'You could serve bar meals,' 'Tried that,' said 'Arry, 'all I sold was pies and not many of them.' 'I'm not surprised', said Ned, tactlessly. 'The one I tried was armour plated. Me teeth were never the same again.'

'Ow about a fun pub?' suggested Charlie .'Get a disco with live groups like the 'Liberty Boat' – to attract the youngsters.' 'Wha?' replied 'Arry, 'the youngsters'd sooner buy cans of lager from the Kut Kost supermarket and then 'ang around by the old people's flats, drinking and causing trouble.'

Charlie drained his glass and banged it down on the bar. Ned did the same, looking hopefully at Charlie. To his disappointment Charlie turned towards the door, 'Some of us have got work to do.' he said. They left 'Arry Wade polishing glasses in his empty pub and muttering what had become his catchphrase in recent times, 'I don't know why I bother.'

'Tell you what, 'said Charlie, getting on his bike, 'I might go down to the 'Liberty Boat' tonight. There's a vintage rock night with live groups – a warm-up for the Easter Festival tomorrow - R&B line dancing, country and western, the lot. D'yer fancy it?' 'What, me?' replied Ned, 'nearest I got to dancin' was one lesson at that dancin' school that used to be behind the cinema. A Spanish feller ran it - well, he said he was Spanish. He started kicking me feet to get them in the right place, so I kicked him back. He didn't sound Spanish after that – didn't dance so good either.'

'Maybe, you're a bit old for it,' said Charlie. 'You're no youngster yourself' replied Ned indignantly. 'Maybe, but I went to the gigs in the sixties. Some of the groups are still playing. The star turn tonight is 'Terry Dactill and the Dinosaurs' don't you remember them?' Charlie shook his head in disbelief 'heavy metal might be more your scene.'

He rode off on his bike leaving Ned rather puzzled by his last remark as he strolled along by the river. He stopped by the small fishing boat dock. Beyond it was the 'Liberty Boat' with its beer garden stretching down to the shore. Tony hailed him from his boat. 'Oy, Ned!' he shouted, 'grab 'old o' dis 'ere rope'. Without further ado he hurled a heavy rope across the dock. It fell on Ned, almost enveloping him. 'Oy, yoy,' laughed Tony, 'You look like bloomin' snake charmer.'

'Thanks very much,' said Ned, struggling to get free from coils of dirty, oily, fish-smelling rope. 'Give us a bit of warning next time.' 'Anyway,' he continued. 'What are all these ropes for? You got the boat tied up like a spider's web.' Tony absently picked a few fish scales off his jersey, 'To keep da' boat in the dock,' he replied, 'not float over the wall.' 'Eh?' said Ned. 'Tonight is very big tide - Easter tide' replied Tony.

'So long, Tony,' said Ned, puzzled by Tony's last remark. What has Easter got to do with the tides? Still, he supposed, Tony must know, he'd earned a precarious living from fishing since he came over as a refugee. He walked past the pub, 'The Liberty Boat'. They've smartened that place up, he thought. It used to be called the 'Blood Boat', or something like that. It had a rough trade off the barges.

The following day Ned took his usual stroll to the 'Boilermakers Arms'. To his surprise the pub was nearly full. Young 'Arry was pulling pints with both hands. Charlie the postman was standing at the bar. 'What're you doing 'ere?' enquired Ned. 'I thought you were going to that Easter festival at 'The Liberty Boat?' 'A sore point that,' replied Charlie in a subdued tone. 'It turned out to be a bit of a turkey.' 'Don't tell me they cancelled it?' said Ned. 'Well, not exactly,' replied Charlie. 'The kids' attractions are going ahead - but they can't sell any ale.' 'Why not?' asked Ned.

'Well,' began Charlie, hesitantly. 'It was last night, see.' 'You mean the rock an' roll show?' asked Ned. 'Yeah, it was great, at least the first half was,' said Charlie.' Terry and the Dinosaurs were doing their spot, everyone was dancing like mad, then they noticed they were splashing in water. Then the electric fused, Terry was jumping like a firecracker and the keyboard went up like a Catherine wheel. You should have seen it.' 'I'm glad I didn't', said Ned, 'What caused it?' 'It was the high tide – flooded the cellar. That's why they can't serve any ale. Half of their regulars are in 'ere.'

Young ' Arry Wade was working harder than he had for years but there was a big smile on his face. 'What I always says,' he said. 'It's an ill wind that blows no good to nobody.'

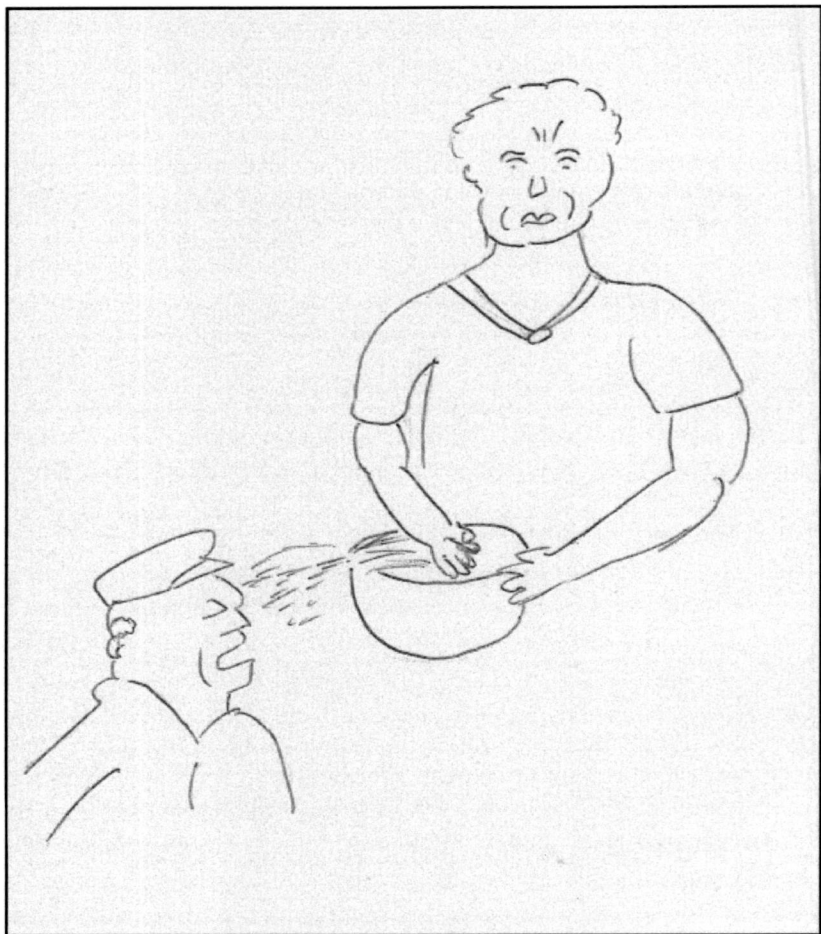

"Try Boiled Rice!"

'Home Help'

Uncle Ned held old-fashioned views concerning his role in the home. He had certain expectations involving regular substantial meals, served when he was ready. The idea of washing dishes, cleaning, cooking or even shopping had never entered his head. Auntie Elsie, on the other hand, had attended sociology classes at the Townswomen's Guild, and was of the opinion that the division of labour in the home needed reforming.

One morning Ned was sitting at the breakfast table reading the racing page of the morning paper. This was his usual routine since he retired from the shipyard. Later, he would saunter down the hill to the betting shop or to the nearest pub, the 'Boilermakers Arms'.

Unfortunately, on that particular day, and not for the first time, he found he was short of money. He asked Elsie for the loan of a 'quid'. 'Where d'you think I get money from?' she snapped. 'It's only 'til this afternoon,' he urged. 'There's a certainty running in the three o clock.' 'A certainty,' she repeated scornfully. 'The only certainty is being thrown out on the street if you waste our pension money on gambling.'

Ned stood up, pulled up his braces and reached for his flat cap.' 'Where d' you think you're going? Elsie continued. 'Out, for a walk', replied Ned in injured tones. 'Well you can make yourself useful,' said Elsie. She thrust a shopping list and a ten pound note into his hand. 'Call at the Kut Kost supermarket while you're at it.'

'Shopping,' said Ned with great dignity, 'is women's work.' 'Oh, is it?' snapped Elsie, 'Well you'd better get used to it, I've slaved for your comfort for long enough. To think I could have married the pawnbroker's son and had a life of luxury.' Ned grabbed his donkey jacket and left. It was no use arguing when Elsie was in that sort of mood.

Ten minutes later he was sipping a pint of bitter in the 'Boilermakers Arms.' 'There's no reasoning with 'er,' he complained. 'She's got this idea that I should be a 'new man' now I've retired. I ask you, how can an old man be a new man?'

'Arry Wade was not paying much attention to Ned. He was staring in amazement at the ten pound note he had just been given. 'You 'ad a win?' he enquired. 'No, that's for shopping. Elsie wants me to go to the Kut Kost supermarket' said Ned.' I'd keep clear if I was you,' advised 'Arry, 'it gets very crowded with shoppers and some of them can get very vicious with their trollies. Me old Dad used to tell me about the battle of the Somme. I never really understood what he meant until I went in that supermarket.'

Ned drained his pint, forgetting for the moment to sip it to make it last. He ordered another pint. 'What about the shopping?' enquired 'Arry as he pulled the pint. 'I'll worry about that later,' replied Ned. 'Don't blame me if you go home with no money, no shopping and smelling of beer,' advised 'Arry. 'Tell you what,' said Ned in a wheedling tone. 'Why don't you put it on old Adam's slate, you know the old bloke who looks after the gardens at the council offices? He owes me a couple of pints for helping 'im.'

'You'll be lucky,' replied 'Arry, 'he lost his job when they turned most of the gardens into a car park. He tried to take them to a tribunal for wrongful dismissal, but they turned him down – said he 'ad insufficient grounds.' Ignoring 'Arry's wheezy laughter, Ned drained his glass and ordered another pint. 'If you're going to spend all your money,' continued 'Arry 'Why don't you eat something while you're 'ere. We do dinners, I mean lunches now.'

'Who've you got cooking 'em?' asked Ned suspiciously. 'The bloke who used to run the bakery down by the railway.' replied 'Arry 'The 'Ealth authority closed his bakery down. People used to call him the 'Cockroach Kid', said Ned 'You'd better go and get your shopping', advised 'Arry in tone that suggested suppressed anger.

Ned finished off another pint and decided to take 'Arry's advice. His money now amounted to a little over two pounds. 'Never mind, eh', he muttered and went straight to the betting shop and placed his money on the certainty in the three o clock race. It lost. Despite the pints of beer he had consumed, Ned was aware that the situation had become desperate. He went back to the pub and pleaded with 'Arry. The landlord was not impressed. He pointed to a notice above the bar, 'no credit, no subs, no cheques cashed'.

Ned, his weatherbeaten face gone strangely pale, spent his last few coppers on a tube of strong mints. 'I can't go 'ome,' he moaned, 'what can I say?' 'What about Goodbye?', suggested 'Arry, unfeelingly. 'Tell you what,' he continued, relenting, 'we've got food left over from dinner, I mean lunch. It'll warm up nicely for tea, I mean evening meal, I mean dinner. Why not bring Elsie in here for a meal on the 'ouse?' Ned crunched a mint thoughtfully, 'Do you think it'd work?' he asked. 'It's your last chance,' replied 'Arry.

When Ned arrived home Elsie was cooking rice. 'You've been a long time,' she remarked. 'Where's the lamb and the sweetcorn and the mushrooms? I'm going to cook a risotto like they showed us at the Townswomen's Guild.' 'Well, 'er, to tell the truth, I didn't fancy that risotto stuff, so I've booked for us to eat out instead.' Elsie looked surprised and pleased. 'Oh, well, she said, that'll make a nice change. You should have said before I cooked the rice.' A look of suspicion crossed her face. 'How did you know I was going to cook a risotto?'

'Oh, well, 'er, I must 'ave guessed,' blustered Ned, very unconvincingly. Elsie sniffed even more suspiciously. 'You smell like a mint factory. You 'avent been drinking again, 'ave you?' 'As if I would,' replied Ned. 'Which restaurant are we going to?' asked Elsie, grim-faced. 'Well, love, all the pubs are starting to serve meals now, and I thought…..' 'The Boilermakers' replied Ned. 'The Boilermakers' said Elsie, her voice rising. 'I wouldn't powder me nose in there. Who've they got cooking for them?' The feller that used to run the bakery,' replied Ned 'You mean the 'Cockroach Kid?' said Elsie in disbelief. 'Yeah,' replied Ned, all hope gone.

There was a pause while Elsie took the pan of rice off the cooker. 'You can put the whole idea out of your mind,' she said, shaking the water off the rice. 'What are we going to eat?' asked Ned. 'Try boiled rice,' replied Elsie, and emptied the pan over him.

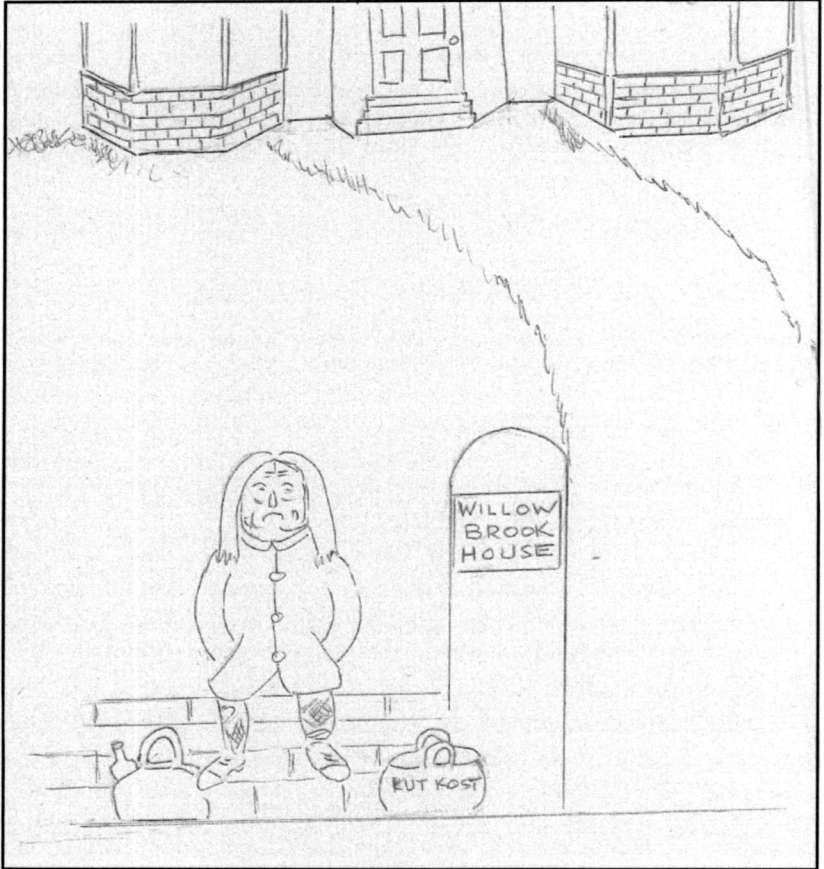

"I want to stay 'ere"

'Desperately seeking Maggie'

One morning in early summer, Uncle Ned was strolling along the bottom road. He passed the betting shop with a visible effort, knowing if he placed a bet, he would probably end up with no money for a drink in the 'Boilermakers Arms.' Such are the agonising choices the retired have to face, he thought, with a glance at the now closed shipyard where he once earned enough money to drink and gamble to his heart's content; that is, if Auntie Elsie didn't get hold of his wage packet first.

It was hot. He loosened his collarless shirt and removed his flat cap. Suddenly, with a rasp of tyres, a post office bike slid to a stop beside him. 'Do us a favour,' gasped Charlie the postman, 'Look out for Methylated Maggie. She's done a bunk, left her flat and gone back to dossing by the look of it.' 'Don't the social services deal with that sort of thing?' asked Ned. 'I phoned 'em up,' replied Charlie, 'Got onto Irma.' His facial expression suggested that it had been a waste of time. 'Who is Irma?' asked Ned. 'The receptionist,' replied Charlie. 'You ask her something and she says, erm, er, I think you've got the wrong number, or something like that.' 'What do I do if I find her?' asked Ned. 'Hang onto her' said Charlie, riding away on his bike. 'What!' muttered Ned, 'the state she'd be in'. But Charlie was half way up the hill.

In Ned's opinion, Charlie's concern for the elderly was a mug's game, especially in the case of Methylated Maggie who had lived rough and scavenged out of bins ever since the war. Against opposition from other residents Charlie had got her a flat, which gave her an address so that she could get benefit. Now it appeared that she had walked away from it. So much for Charlie's efforts. He always had been a soft touch.

Ned had intended to have a word with some old cronies, the racing experts who sat in the park, but, remembering that he owed Charlie a favour or two, he turned towards the river. Passing the dock he was hailed by Tony. 'Oy, Ned,' he shouted from his boat. 'You come for trip, catch conger eel?' 'No thanks Tony,' replied Ned quickly, 'I'm looking for Methylated Maggie.' Tony picked a few fish scales from his jersey. 'Pooh, she stink,' he said.' She come for cat fish.' 'She's got no cat,' replied Ned. 'Cat wouldn't eat what I give her.' said Tony.

Ned looked at the murky channels and mudbanks. A thought occurred to him. 'Hey, you don't suppose?' he began. 'Gone For a swim?' suggested Tony, 'Oy yoy, she got her pension yesterday. She'll be sleeping it off.' 'Where?' asked Ned. 'Ask the skipper,' said Tony. 'Who?' 'Another dosser, like Maggie,' said Tony, 'they call him that because he sleeps in the skips.'

With Tony's strange laugh still ringing in his ears Ned wandered back through the skip dump. He saw no sign of life except for a rat scuttling through the rubbish. He felt hot, tired and thirsty as the turned towards the 'Boilermakers Arms'. Before he had gone very far, Charlie came pedalling along. 'Any luck?' he called. Ned shook his head, 'I'm going for a pint,' he said . 'I'll come with you,' said Charlie, 'I'll even buy you one, but first I want to check if Maggie is hanging around by the Gospel Hall.'

The Gospel Hall was half way up the hill leading to the town's better-off residential district. It looked deserted, locked up, closed. A few tattered notices clung to the door. One handwritten one asked, 'Come to Sunday worship and bring a fiend with you.' 'That's why it closed,' said Ned. They walked up the hill past large Edwardian-style houses, some of which looked neglected. It was hot. Ned took his jacket off. 'Let's go and get that pint,' Ned suggested with a note of pleading.

'Wait a minute,' said Charlie peering up the road. 'There's someone, sitting on a garden wall. I think it's her.' Methylated Maggie sat facing a large, stone-built mansion known as 'Willowbrook House'. Beside her were two carrier bags. 'Looks like she's left 'ome for good', said Charlie. 'But why has she come 'ere?' asked Ned. 'Some of the lads

I worked with used to say it's haunted.'

'Come on home,' said Charlie to Maggie. 'Got no home,' said Maggie dejectedly, 'I've been bombed out.' 'Don't you mean burgled?' said Charlie. 'No, that was at the flat,' she replied.' Charlie tapped his forehead. 'Come on, we're wasting our time.' 'Wait a minute' said Ned thoughtfully. 'I remember something about this house. The first bomb of the war fell here, - direct hit on the air raid shelter in the garden. The whole family was killed; all except a little servant girl too frightened to leave the attic.'

'What a tragedy.' exclaimed Charlie. 'Yeah,' agreed Ned, 'it was one of them corrugated iron shelters. They all got decapitated.' 'Spare us the details,' said Charlie with a shudder. 'Anyway, we can't stay 'ere all day. 'I want to stay' said Maggie. 'You mean, you want to stay in this house?' said Charlie,' I want to stay,' repeated Maggie, firmly.

Charlie looked thoughtful. 'Go back to your flat for a day or two and I'll do what I can to fix it for you to live here. Will you do that?' She nodded. Charlie turned to Ned. 'I think that's one problem solved,' he continued hopefully. 'Let's go and get that pint.' As they turned to go they passed a faded notice board. It read, 'Willowbrook Residential Home for the Elderly.'

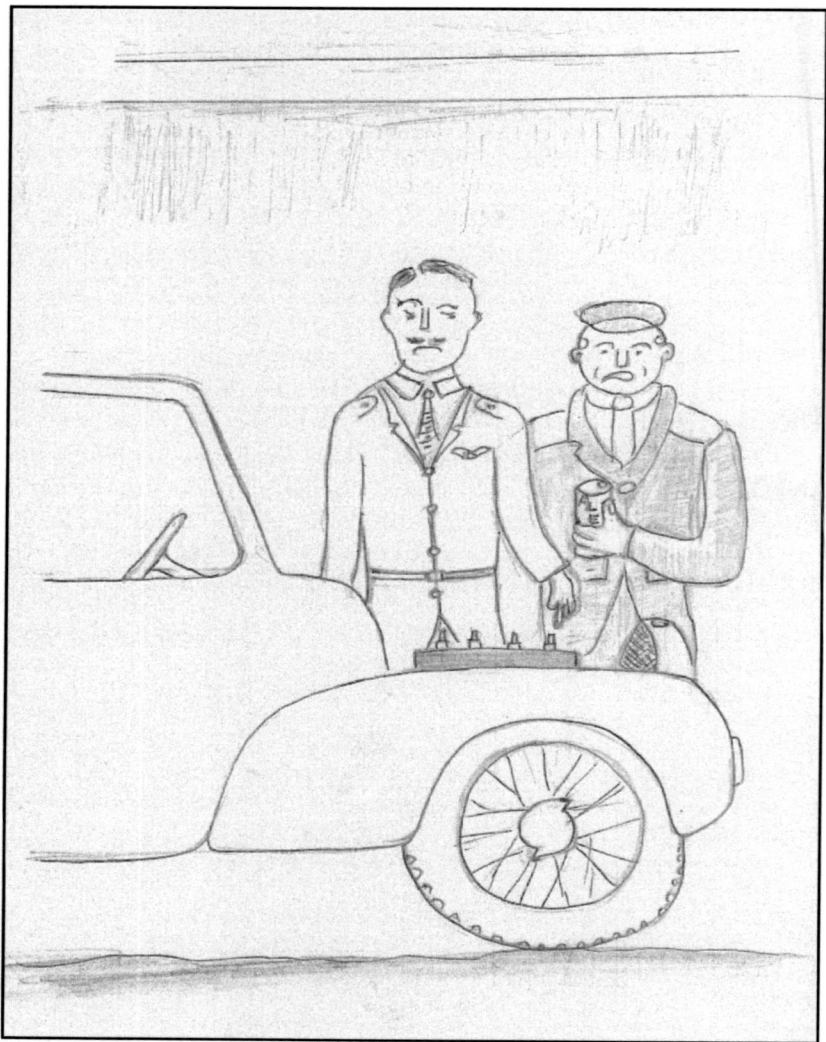

Ready for the Lift

'Something Fishy in the Woodyard'

Uncle Ned always had a strong sense of what was fair and proper. If anyone bought him a drink he always bought one back, except when he was broke, which, come to think of it was fairly often, especially after he retired. Even then, he would try to find some way to return the favour. However he was not altogether pleased when Charlie the postman asked him to help repair his car. He felt that he could not refuse as he had accepted several lifts from Charlie, not to mention several pints in the 'Boilermakers Arms'.

Auntie Elsie told him to refuse point blank. 'I know what'll happen. You'll strain your back, get covered with grease and perished with cold in that miserable lock-up garage.'

Ned walked out, mumbling that 'he couldn't let a mate down.' He was soon at the bar of the pub enjoying a pint provided by Charlie as advance payment, as Ned saw it. Charlie was full of enthusiasm about his car which he said was a 'classic'. Ned thought of it as a 'banger' but tactfully kept silent. Charlie chatted on about the repairs he intended to carry out on the engine which, he said, it would enable the car to reach speeds of over forty miles an hour. By closing time, Ned had almost fallen asleep from boredom.

The next day was bleak and cold, hardly an ideal day for removing a car engine, but at least it was dry. Charlie the postman had completed his round in record time, even so it was twilight before they could begin work on the car. While Charlie probed under the car's bonnet with a dim lead lamp, Ned found his attention wandering. The yard or compound where the lock-up garages and small business huts stood had been a quarry in the past, long before Ned's time. He remembered it as a scrap wood yard, run by an old man who had died some time ago. On many a fine summer evening Ned had paused on his way home from the pub to chat with the old man. Some of his tales had been of a strange and eerie nature. Ned had laughed at the time but now, with the black quarry wall looming over them, those tales did not seem so funny.

'Right, Ned,' called Charlie, 'I've disconnected the engine. All we've got to do is to lift it out.' Ned looked at the oily mass, 'Lift it out?' he said. 'Yeah,' replied Charlie, 'Lift it out?' said Ned uncertainly, 'Can't we borrow a whatsitsname from Fred at the Tool Hire shop?' 'I borrowed his hoist when I changed the shock absorbers,' replied Charlie. 'What happened?' asked Ned. 'It bent,' said Charlie,' a bit of work'll warm us up. Anyway, you're a strong bloke.'

'Aye,' agreed Ned, pleased with the description, 'Mind you,' he added, 'since I finished at the shipyard, I've lifted nothing heavier than a pint.' He pulled his wide leather belt a notch tighter and took hold of the engine. 'One two, lift,' called Charlie. The engine moved an inch or two. 'An' again,' he croaked, his arms stretching like an orang-utan's. 'Lift!'

With that last desperate heave the engine came out. Gasping for breath, Ned straightened his back, glad that he could still do so, and that his reputation as 'a strong bloke' was still intact. 'What about going for a pint?' he suggested. 'I don't reckon we'd be welcome in the 'Boilermakers' covered in oil and dust,' replied Charlie. ''Arry's trying to make the place a bit up market, serving meals an' all.' 'I 'eard about it,' said Ned with a note of disgust. 'In the old days he'd serve a pint and a pie to anyone. A bit of oil, rust or red lead used to improve the flavour. Did you hear they had to call the ambulance the other day? Somebody choked.' 'On the food?' asked Charlie, 'No, on the bill,' said Ned.

Charlie wiped his hands on a rag. He rummaged in the back of the car. 'Here you are,' he said, 'best canned bitter.' 'Better than nowt, I suppose,' said Ned doubtfully. 'got a can opener?' 'You just pull the ring,' said Charlie. 'What will they think of next?' said Ned. But after two or three cans he was pulling rings as to the manor born. Charlie was again burbling on about his plans to restore the car to concourse condition. 'What do you mean, conkers?' said Ned. Before Charlie could answer, a rattling noise attracted their attention.

'Hush! There's somebody here,' whispered Charlie nervously. 'It's the old man and his dog,' suggested Ned, hiding a grin. 'He's dead isn't he?' asked Charlie. 'Oh aye, so he is,' replied Ned. 'You know, he told me Spring-heeled Jack used to haunt this place.' 'There's a funny smell here,' said Charlie, 'like fish.' 'The old man told me there was a fish market here years ago, before the river was banked up,' said Ned 'It's only them kids,' said Charlie, 'they come around at this time o' year – trick or treat.'

Just as Charlie and Ned had reassured themselves that they weren't being haunted, a high-pitched cackle of laughter startled them. It seemed to come from under the quarry wall. 'That's not kids,' said Ned. 'Sounded like an old woman to me,' replied Charlie nervously. 'Perhaps it's the ghost of one of the fish sellers' said Ned, 'The old man said they used to get up to some tricks. If you didn't buy their fish they'd hit you with one.'

'Don't talk daft,' said Charlie scornfully, 'that's no ghost, who else could it be but Methylated Maggie?' 'Yeah, agreed Ned, 'but, wait a minute, isn't she in that old people's home 'Wilderness House' or whatever they call it?'

'So she is,' agreed Charlie, 'but the Matron told me she's always trying to get out and go back to her old ways. I'll go to 'Willowbrook House' tomorrow and have a word with the Matron. Let's get out of here before we die of cold, or fright.'

The next day, Charlie, while on his round, called at the residential home where Methylated Maggie had finally found some comfort after years of scrounging and sleeping rough. To his surprise, he was told that Maggie was unwell: proper food seemed to disagree with her. She had been kept in bed for the past couple of days.

Uncle Ned catches the bottle

'The League of Friends'

'What we want on the committee,' said Charlie the postman, straightening his back with an effort, 'are folks who aren't frightened of a bit of work.'

'Don't look at me,' said Ned, wiping his bald head with a large handkerchief. 'I've only come to give a hand, not to join a committee.' He returned to his job of digging the neglected flower beds in front of 'Willowbrook House', the local residential home for the elderly. 'This is not much easier than working at the shipyard and I got paid for that,' he grumbled. 'I do it for nowt and I'm not even retired yet,' said Charlie. 'Someone's got to help out, I mean, we'll all be old some day.'

After another ten minutes or so of digging Ned enquired if it was time to go to the pub. Charlie was not listening, as he was extracting a bottle from under the shrubbery. 'Blimey!' exclaimed Ned, 'a half-full bottle of whisky. We don't need to go to the pub. The pub's come to us.' 'Ow do we know it's whisky?' said Charlie dubiously, 'want to try it?' 'No thanks,' replied Ned, his enthusiasm dying away, 'who the 'eck hides whisky bottles in the garden?' 'Methylated Maggie who else? I've found 'em before,' said Charlie.

Later, after some refreshment at the 'Boilermakers Arms', Ned arrived home. Auntie Elsie regarded him with suspicion. 'Where've you been?' she said. 'Gardening at Willowbrook House', he replied. 'Oh, aye', said Elsie, you smell like a brewery.' 'Ask Charlie if you don't believe me,' replied Ned, 'he wants me to join the League of Friends.'

'What, you?' she said in disbelief, 'you aren't going to, are you?' 'Why not?' replied Ned. 'You'd be useless.' said Elsie. 'I'll show you,' replied Ned, stung. 'I'll go to the next meeting and see what it's like.' 'I'll believe that when it happens,' said Elsie.

The next meeting of the 'Willowbrook House' League of Friends was an Annual General Meeting and dinner. It took place in the residents lounge, cleared for the occasion. The Chairman was Mr Denham, the old soldier from the flats wearing his regimental tie. 'Why's he in charge?' asked Ned. 'Nobody else wanted the job,' said Charlie. Mr Denham opened the meeting. 'We have to appoint a Secretary,' he declared in his clipped voice. The conversations stopped in mid-sentence. Nobody volunteered. 'I wish my batman was here.' said Mr Denham. 'Batman,' exclaimed Ned. 'Are we going to play cricket?' 'No,' explained Charlie patiently,' he means his servant, his back-up man.' 'He gets everybody's back up,' said Ned, 'anyway, how come he had a servant?' 'He was an officer, for a short while', replied Charlie 'I heard he marched his troops straight into an enemy camp. When they let him come home after the war they cashiered him.' 'That sounds painful' said Ned. 'Keep silence at the back there.' barked Mr Denham.

'Sorry, yer Honour', said Ned. This was ignored as the Matron sat down at the top table. 'I'll take the minutes,' she said. 'You can't,' replied Mr Denham, 'you're ex-officio.' At this the Assistant Matron stood up. 'Don't you dare speak to the Matron like that. She's as much officio as you are, you self-important bag of wind.'

'That's telling 'im,' laughed Charlie, 'She's a terror, that one. The residents call her 'Vinegar.' Mr Denham's face turned brick-red above his white moustache. 'If that's the way you behave', he spluttered. 'By Jove, I'll close the meeting right now.' There was a roar of approval and shouts of 'Bring on the dinner, we're starving 'ere.'

'I thought this was supposed to be a League of Friends,' said Ned above the noise. 'It don't seem very friendly to me.' 'Now calm down,' said the Matron, effectively taking charge. The din subsided. 'There's no need for all that. I'm sure Lavinia did not mean you to take offence.'

After the initial delay, business proceeded quite rapidly. Charlie soon found himself re-elected and Ned elected, both unanimously and without opposition, and they were thanked for their previous good work. The Matron made her report in which she mentioned some problems, mainly the disappearance of some petty cash, and the finding of several bottles in the garden. She also mentioned two difficult residents, Norman and Maggie. The former, known as 'Big Norman' was aggressive and uncooperative, while the latter, known as 'Methylated Maggie' was a sad case who had spent most of her life homeless, but was harmless and put-upon by other residents.

Some of the members were near to tears as the business part of the meeting ended, whether from sympathy or from hunger wasn't clear. Ned was glad to get on with dinner. Despite his unfamiliarity with formal dining he only made one mistake; he put horseradish sauce on his fish course and tartare sauce on his beef. However he said 'it tasted great'. He was annoyed when someone hogged all the cheese and biscuits, but when the Chairman called for everyone to charge their glasses for the toast, he said he'd have the toast instead.

The following day, despite a mild hangover, Ned arrived at 'Willowbrook House' to finish digging the flower beds. He had scarcely begun when a figure approached, small, bandy, red-faced and brandishing an empty whisky bottle. It was 'Methylated Maggie'. 'You rotten swine,' she yelled, 'you shopped me to the Matron.' Ned protested his innocence, but all that did was to provoke a stream of foul abuse that left Ned, a life-long shipyard worker, shocked and speechless. Maggie swung back her arm and hurled the bottle with tremendous force straight at Ned's head. Only the reflexes he had developed as a youth, catching red-hot rivets in a glove, saved him. He retreated to the gate, rapidly.

'Harmless did she say?' he muttered. 'Flippin' 'eck, I'd sooner take on 'Big Norman.'

"Better than Bitter"

'Maggie's Party'

Charlie the postman was looking distracted and absent-minded. He stood at the bar of the 'Boilermakers Arms' and bought pints of bitter for himself and Uncle Ned, forgetful of the fact that he had bought the previous round. 'I'm worried about Methylated Maggie,' he said. 'You've only got yourself to blame,' replied Ned. 'You got her a flat and she got into a lot of trouble – then you got her into a residential home.' 'Aye, and she's got herself into a load of trouble there,' said Charlie gloomily. 'Once a dosser, always a dosser,' said Ned in a superior tone that irritated Charlie. 'Come on Ned, be fair, I mean, the poor old so and so was bombed out when she was no more than a kid.' 'Er and 'undreds of others. They didn't all start sleepin' rough,' replied Ned.

'The war was a bad time for everybody,' said Charlie , seriously. Ned gave a scornful laugh. 'What d' you know about it?' You where still in short trousers when it started.' Charlie drew himself up and pointed to his blazer badge. 'I did National Service,' he said. 'National Service!' sneered Ned. 'The only action you saw was at the camp cinema.' A silence fell. Ned suspected he had gone too far. He was sure of it when Charlie bought another pint of bitter and didn't include him. 'I do admire the work you do for the poor and needy,' he said. ' If you need 'elp , just count on me.' 'Now you're talking,' said Charlie, 'what'll you 'ave?'

The Matron at 'Willowbrook House' was basically a kind person but even her patience was not inexhaustible. 'Look here,

Maggie,' she said firmly. 'Nobody said you're in prison. You can go out, so long as you let me know. You seem to forget that we're responsible for you now.' 'I can look after meself,' said Maggie. 'You're too old for staying out all night like you did last week. You'll be seventy on your next birthday,' said the Matron. 'If you behave yourself we'll have a party for you.' She did not mention that all the residents were given a party on their birthdays.

'A Party, eh?' said Maggie, 'Can I invite a few friends and get some bottles in?' 'I'll have to think about the friends, and definitely no bottles,' replied the Matron. A few days later, Charlie the postman was surprised to be stopped on his round by the Matron. 'We are having a party next week for Maggie' she said, 'It's for her seventieth birthday but she wants to invite friends and bring in drink. The drink is out of course and I'm a bit dubious about her friends. She wants you and Ned to come, I'd be glad if you could – in case things get out of hand.' 'I'll do me best to be there,' said Charlie. 'I can't answer for Ned, seeing there's no drink allowed, but I'll ask him.'

A birthday party was a major event in the lives of the residents. Those who were capable had dressed up for the occasion. The guests sat in a self-conscious group near the door. Apart from Charlie and Ned, there was Tony the fisherman and a silent young man dressed in a black anorak with the hood up. Tony leaned over and whispered to Ned. 'Dey call him the Skipper.' 'Eh?' replied Ned, unable to understand Tony's mid-European accent. Tony gestured to Ned to come closer. 'You know der yard by the dock where all de skips are? Well, 'e sleeps in dem.' Ned nodded vigorously, edging away from Tony's jersey, which smelt strongly of fish.

The Matron asked the young man, who was rolling a cigarette from a tin of wiry-looking tobacco, if he would like to take his anorak off. He declined with a shake of his head. 'He's a clever fellow,' whispered Charlie to Ned. 'Who? Tony?' replied Ned. 'No, the Skipper. 'He applied for a job teaching Mathematics,' said Charlie. 'Did he get it?' asked Ned. 'No', replied Charlie, 'they told him he shouldn't count on it.'

Ned looked around the room. 'Are these all the friends Maggie's got?' he asked. 'She told me she's got a few more but they ain't so, what did she say? socially accomplished,' replied Charlie. 'Blimey', said Ned. The Matron produced a cake with seven candles on it. 'We couldn't get seventy on the cake, dear,' she said. 'There'd be a fire 'azard,' muttered Ned.

Maggie seemed to become shy, and had to be persuaded to blow out the candles. As the Matron was cutting up the cake on the table, Maggie moved furtively towards the sideboard upon which stood a large teapot. She fumbled with the front of her dress which was looking slightly misshapen, as though it was concealing something. Could it be a bottle?

After the tea was passed around, a certain conviviality became noticeable. The guests loosened up and began to socialise with the residents, many of whom were normally very quiet. A party spirit developed in which reminiscences were exchanged and jokes told. An old man gave a solo performance on the spoons and Big Norman offered to arm-wrestle anyone for a ten bob bet. Methylated Maggie surprised everyone with a very good rendition of "There's No Place like Home".

The Matron called an end to the proceedings after Tony began a peasant dance that involved leaping and squatting and shouting 'Hoy!'. The more nervous of the residents retreated in panic, but Tony did receive one compliment. The young man in the anorak broke his silence to declare it 'Great'.

Going down the drive, Ned had the impression that the gateposts had moved to the left, but when he adjusted the direction of his walk, they moved to the right. 'You know, Charlie.' He said, 'that tea was good stuff. It was better than bitter.' Unfortunately, he had a problem pronouncing the last few words. 'Yer right,' agreed Charlie, 'batter than butter.'

Ned lowers the tone

'Book Launch'

Auntie Elsie was unusually quiet over breakfast, so much so that even Uncle Ned noticed. 'Somethin' up' love?,' he asked, buttering a round of toast as though he was spreading plaster. 'Didn't sleep very well,' she replied. 'someone was snoring like a pneumatic drill.' 'Wonder who that was,' said Ned, refilling his teacup for the third time. 'It wasn't Clark Gable,' retorted Elsie, regarding Ned with distaste.

Noticing her glance, Ned buttoned up his collarless shirt and pulled his dangling braces over his shoulders. 'You can 'ave a lie down later on', he said solicitously, 'when you've finished the washing and cleaning and all that.' 'Very kind of you, I'm sure,' replied Elsie, 'but I've got more to do than lying down. The Townswomen's Guild are having a book launch this afternoon at the Library and I said I'd help out.'

'Oh, aye,' replied Ned, only half listening, 'I always liked to watch a launch when I worked in the shipyard. I used to feel sad.' 'You mean, sad to see the ship leave after all the work you'd done on it?' asked Elsie. 'No,' replied Ned. 'It was all that waste of champagne.' 'Go on, clear off,' said Elsie impatiently. Snatching a last round of toast, Ned left. He knew when he was not wanted.

Ned walked down the entry behind the houses, his hobnailed boots clumping on the flagstones. It was a chilly day with a threat of rain in the wind, not a good day for hanging around the park. He pulled the peak of his flat cap down and the collar of his donkey jacket up, wondering if he could shelter in the betting shop or the pub. The trouble with that was, apart from some small change, he had no money. He headed for the last resort left, the Library.

Uncle Ned

The Library was an old-fashioned building with glazed partitions and a ticking clock. Beyond the bookshelves was a reading area with all the daily newspapers spread out on a table. Several elderly men sat hunched over the papers, usually studying the sports pages. The Librarian, an elderly thin-faced woman glanced at the men from time to time, her expression conveyed the wish that newspapers should be read standing up, and people merely passing the time should be asked to leave, a situation that had existed until fairly recently.

Ned looked round at the other men. They met every day, like a sort of informal club to study the racing page-in the park if the weather was fair. Ned looked out of the window and noticed that a drizzle had set in. He decided to stay put. The Librarian came slowly along the bookshelves pushing a trolley full of books that she slammed into the shelves noisily. Ned fought down an inclination to say 'Shush.'

'Are you men here to choose books?' asked the Librarian sharply. She addressed Ned. 'Do you need any help?' Ned was momentarily taken aback. He felt about five years old and nearly called her Miss. 'I -er - forgot me ticket,' he said at last. 'There are some books for sale over by the door,' said the Librarian, 'perhaps you'd like to look.'

Ned got up to look at the books, unable to think of any reason not to. He felt defeated. Thumbing through the old novels and dated information books, he saw that they were priced quite cheaply and decided to buy one for Elsie. Handing over his twenty pence to the Librarian, he received another verbal shot. 'You men will have to move away from this area shortly. A book launch is to take place here this afternoon.' Ned drew himself up to his full five foot six. 'Yes, I know,' he said. 'Me missus, I mean my wife, is one of the horganisers.' Ned had the satisfaction of seeing the Librarian's grim face bow slightly in defeat.

By now a couple of men had arrived and were setting out chairs at the back of the library. Soon the members of the Guild, mostly large, middle-aged ladies, began to arrive. Ned took a seat at the side of the rear row, as far out of sight as possible.

The President of the Guild, a lady even larger than the others, introduced the guest speaker, a retired schoolmaster and local historian. At the other side of the table, next to a large pile of new books, sat Elsie who appeared to be acting as Secretary.

The schoolmaster, who was the author, began describing the contents of the book, mainly a compilation of historical facts, most of them unknown to Ned who had been born and brought up in the area. On the other hand, Ned knew a few facts that the schoolmaster didn't but, as these were rough and ready tales, he kept quiet.

The Library was hot. The schoolmaster droned on. Ned began to drift into sleep. He awoke to hear, 'there used to be many more public houses per head of population than there are now. The oldest was not the 'Boilermakers Arms' as is generally supposed but the "Old Flat" in Unity Street. That notorious hostelry had to close when the owner lost his licence for selling beer to minors.' Ned gave a loud guffaw, 'Them miners'd sup ale from a sweaty clog.'

A silence fell. 'Who is that?' asked the schoolmaster. 'An old tramp,' replied the President. Elsie recognised Ned for the first time. Her jaw fell open, her eyes protruded and her face went bright red. Ned, on the other hand went pale. He awaited his chance to slip out without attracting further attention. This came when the guest speaker concluded his talk and the President announced an interval. While the members were jostling to pay four pounds ninety-nine for each book from a harassed Elsie, Ned made his escape.

He went straight home. Using his best culinary skills, he prepared the tea before Elsie arrived. It was his specialité de la maison, beans on toast. The rattle of the front door almost made him drop the pan of beans. Elsie came in with a face of fury. 'Why do you always show me up?' she shouted, 'every time I try to do something civilised.' 'Sorry love,' replied Ned, juggling with a piece of hot toast that he was trying to butter. 'I didn't know you was goin' to be there.' 'I told you,' she snapped, her voice rising dangerously, 'I told you this morning. You never listen. I may as well talk to the table.' She hit it for emphasis. Ned dropped the toast.

'I got your tea ready,' he said ingratiatingly,' and I got you a book.' 'Where did you get four pounds ninety-nine to pay for it?' asked Elsie. 'Er, it was a bit cheaper than that,' replied Ned, showing her the book. 'How to cure insomnia,' she read from the cover. 'What use is that to me?' 'Well, you said this morning you couldn't sleep,' said Ned.

The next day Elsie had got over her anger. She was, on reflection, thankful that none of the ladies of the Guild had recognised the 'old tramp' as her husband. She even complimented Ned on his choice of book. 'I read one page of it in bed,' she said, 'and I went fast asleep for the rest of the night.'

Waiting for service

'The Visit'

One morning Uncle Ned was lingering at the breakfast table, reading the racing page of the local paper. He had finished his grilled bacon on toast which was the nearest he could get to a good fry-up since Elsie had become obsessive about healthy eating after attending a lecture at the Townswomen's Guild. His request for fried bread was refused point blank but she allowed him to dollop tomato sauce over his bacon. He wondered why Elsie was so indulgent. He was usually ejected into the street before now. 'Annie's coming to stay for a few days,' announced Elsie suddenly.

'When?' gasped Ned when he had finished choking on his tea. 'Tomorrow,' replied Elsie, as Ned slumped back in horror. 'You'll have to smarten yourself up.' Ten minutes later, Ned, dressed in his flat cap and donkey jacket was in the 'Boilermakers Arms' confiding sorrowfully to the landlord 'Arry Wade. ''Ard luck,' replied 'Arry, I remember her well. Didn't she marry a fish fryer?' 'Yeah, old Jack Wood, she became Annie Wood,' continued Ned. ' She only comes to stay with us once in a while like 'Allys comet - but when she does everybody knows about it.'

'I reckon old Jack thought she was soft like, thought she'd slave over a big fish and chip pan,' said 'Arry, 'but pretty soon he found out different.' 'Some 'opes,' said Ned. 'Elsie's pretty tough but Annie's got a degree in it, a bloomin' P.HD.' 'Old Jack 'ad a lot to learn,' said 'Arry. 'Some people said 'e battered her, but it wasn't long before 'e'd had 'is chips.' 'Arry cackled with laughter. 'I reckoned there was something fishy about it,' he added clinging to the beer pump for support. Ned regarded him with distaste. 'It's all right for you. I've got to face her tomorrow' he said. 'Like one of them gladiators in ancient Rome,' said 'Arry. 'We who are about to die, salute you.' 'Arry gave another burst of wheezy laughter. Ned drained his pint and left.

The following day, Elsie made Ned wear a cotton shirt and a tie instead of his usual collarless garment. His stained flat cap was hidden away as were his hobnailed boots. He sat like a condemned man waiting for the knock at the front door. This came soon enough as a taxi deposited Auntie Annie outside on the pavement. 'Bring the cases in,' ordered Elsie. Ned picked up the two suitcases, his arms stretching like an orang-utan's. 'What's she got in 'ere?' he muttered, 'weight training equipment?'

Annie sat down in Ned's chair with a gasp. 'It's a hard life being a widow,' she exclaimed to nobody in particular. Her hair was dyed jet black and framed her withered face. Ned was reminded of something he had once seen in a museum, a shrunken head. 'Take my cases to my room,' she said to Ned. 'Yes Ma'am,' he replied. As he went up the stairs he heard Annie ask Elsie why she had married him instead of the pawnbroker's son. He heard Elsie reply, 'I must have been barmy.'

The rest of the afternoon passed quickly enough for the two sisters as they drank endless cups of tea and exchanged news. To Ned the day seemed endless. At teatime, Elsie produced one of her organically-grown salads.

'What do you call that?' asked Annie with a forced laugh. 'Healthy eating,' replied Elsie. 'It's good for you.' 'For you, maybe,' said Annie. 'I've been travelling half the day.'

Ned, though not particularly sensitive, could feel the tension building up. Unwisely, he opened his mouth for the first time that afternoon. 'I could go for some fish and chips,' he suggested. Elsie kicked him under the table. 'I wouldn't dream of putting you to any trouble.' Said Annie, icily 'Elsie is quite right. We should all eat healthy food regularly. I suggest once a year.'

The following day Annie decided to treat Elsie to a restaurant meal. Somewhat reluctantly, she included Ned in the arrangement. The object may have been to avoid another one of Elsie's healthy meals, but to be fair, Annie was not mean. She had money left to her by her late husband and liked to live in style. She chose the most expensive restaurant in town. Ned would have preferred to have gone to the cafeteria by the docks. His idea of dining out was not so much Egon Ronay, more egg on chips.

The place was full. The waiter, a middle-aged man in immaculate formal dress, told them rather haughtily that there were no tables available. Ned and Elsie turned to go, but not Annie. 'What about that table?' she snapped, pointing to one where the customers were preparing to leave. 'That's reserved,' replied the waiter. 'If you wish to dine here it is advisable to book in advance.' Ned and Elsie again turned to leave. The waiter walked away but Annie's piercing voice made him turn back. 'What time?' she enquired loudly. 'Pardon?' said the waiter, a look of astonishment on his face. 'What time is that table booked for?' demanded Annie. 'Er, nine o clock I believe.' replied the waiter, his composure crumbling a little. 'It's only seven now, we'll be finished by then' said Annie firmly as she led the way to the table and sat down. After a while the waiter cleared and re-set the table. He did not look pleased. He handed a menu to Ned and left without a word.

Annie snatched the menu from Ned and scanned it with practised ease and decided on her order. Elsie who had learned a little about continental cooking, the dishes of which were listed in French, managed to make her choice. Ned was completely lost. He could not even choose a starter. 'What about a paté or a mousse?' suggested Elsie. 'I thought pate was the top of your 'ed,' he said, staring blankly at the menu, 'and I'm not eating anything with mouse in it.' Ordering the main course was just as difficult. 'What's this tournedos like?' he asked. 'Does it give you wind?' Eventually, after much embarrassment, they had their orders ready.

After what seemed a long time, the waiter returned and took their orders in an offhand manner. When Annie ordered a bottle of Beaujolais he brought it to the table and uncorked it. When Annie mentioned that red wine needed time to breath, he said it would have plenty before the meal was ready. Ned asked for a pint of bitter and was kicked under the table by Elsie. Ignoring Ned's request for beer, the waiter poured some of the wine and handed the glass to Ned to taste, even though it was quite apparent that Ned was out of his depth. He took a large gulp of the wine, choked and said, 'Blimey, it tastes like pi....Ow,' he rubbed his other leg where Elsie had kicked him, 'I was only going to say it tastes like pickled cabbage.'

The waiter paid them no further attention. Another half hour passed while he ushered customers to other tables, took their orders and served them. Annie got very angry. 'I'm going to speak to him,' she hissed. 'Don't make a scene for goodness sake,' pleaded Elsie. 'Leave this to me,' said Ned suddenly. Annie sat open-mouthed with surprise as Ned got up, walked to the door from the kitchen and blocked it just as the waiter was coming out. 'I want a word with you,' said Ned. 'What about?' asked the waiter angrily, 'you'd better make it quick, I'm busy.' His refined accent had begun to slip. 'You know what it's about, you're ignoring us,' replied Ned, 'you were just as awkward when you were an apprentice at the shipyard. I remember when you wouldn't make the tea –thought it was beneath your bloomin' dignity –until I clipped you across the ear.'

The man's jaw dropped. He peered at Ned, then his face broke into a smile. 'Well, if it ain't old Ned. I didn't recognise you in a suit and tie. Sit down, mate, and I'll serve you right away.' He did too. They enjoyed a superb meal, served by a very attentive and polite waiter. Ned was even provided with a pint of beer.

Some days later, after Annie had gone home, Ned told Elsie how the problem in the restaurant had been solved. Auntie Annie never knew, but afterwards, she treated Ned with a lot more respect.

"Which Doctor?"

'The Patient'

Uncle Ned considered himself fit for his age. Although he had been retired from the shipyard for several years, he had not gained any weight, in fact he had become slimmer. This was probably because he drank less ale, not because of any deliberate reform, but because he had less money.

In his local pub, the 'Boilermakers Arms' he had a long-standing reputation as a tough character. He was quite happy to demonstrate his still considerable strength by helping out shifting barrels or by lifting machinery at the Tool Hire shop, providing there was a pint or two at the end of it.

Consequently, he wondered why he had to stop and recover his breath on the way home from the pub. In his prime he had negotiated the steep hill even after one of his legendary binges without any problem whilst some of his workmates were weaving about, zig-zag fashion and others could scarcely walk at all.

When he confided his anxiety to Auntie Elsie, he met with scant sympathy. 'It's the food you eat, chips with every meal and fried breakfasts every day. You don't listen to me. They said at the Guild somebody has a heart attack every three minutes.' 'That poor bloke must be in an 'eck of a state.' 'You know what I mean, replied Elsie angrily, from now on you'll eat more salad and less fatty food.' 'I can't live on that,' said Ned, 'what d'yer think I am, eh? a bloomin' rabbit?'

Ned clutched his cap and headed towards the door. 'Now where are you going?' said Elsie. 'To the doctors', said Ned. 'Don't go near that chip shop,' called Elsie. It was not the first time Ned had gone for a health check. In spite of having suffered nothing worse than a cold or a minor injury at work, he always thought that any minor disorder was the start of a fatal disease. Auntie Elsie called him a hypochondriac, which led him to declare that there was no pretence about him. This was true but puzzling, until Elsie realised he thought she meant hypocrite.

Reaching the doctor's surgery, Ned noticed that two new names had been added to the brass plate. The surgery was now a group practice. The receptionist was new too. 'Which doctor?' she asked. 'I 'aven't come here to see a witch doctor,' replied Ned, 'I want to see Doctor Knowles.'

The receptionist's face was a picture. 'This town's full of comedians,' she confided to her colleague, an elderly woman with orange-dyed hair who was rattling the keyboard of a computer, cursing at her mistakes and peering at the screen as though she couldn't believe what she was seeing.

'Yer gorra be a comedian to live 'ere,' said Ned, picking up a paper slip with a number on it, 'Blimey! Just like the Social Security,' he added.' I remember you,' said the older receptionist, turning away from the computer screen that had just gone blank. 'Last time you came in 'ere you were rude to Doctor Knowles.' 'Well, he was rude to me,' retorted Ned indignantly. 'All I did was to ask him what you were supposed to do with suppositories. And do you know what he said?' 'We don't want to know,' said the first receptionist. 'Join the queue over there.'

Ned sat down beside another elderly man who was shifting about on his chair. 'Got to go to the toilet,' he said, 'it's them pills the Doc gave me. Don't take any. I spend half me time passing water.' The receptionist called, 'Next', and the man got up. 'Hang on a minute,' said Ned. 'What are they called, the pills?' The man paused and looked around as though he was giving Ned secret information. 'Niagara,' he said.

By the time Ned arrived home it was mid-afternoon, the time when Ned usually took a nap. Elsie was anxious in case one or more of her friends from the Townswomen's Guild might turn up and see Ned lying on the settee. 'There's tea in the pot,' Elsie said, half expecting him to decline the offer as he usually did if he had come from the pub. This time he took a cup eagerly. 'I've been to the doctor's. I thought I'd never get out.' said Ned. 'What did he say?' asked Elsie, a note of concern in her voice. 'He put a strap around me arm and pumped it up. I thought me hand was going to fall off.' 'What did he say?' repeated Elsie. 'He said I've got to watch me cholera or something.' said Ned. 'You mean cholesterol, not cholera, cholera's fatal' said Elsie. 'Blimey' exclaimed Ned.

He sat sipping his tea thoughtfully, 'There's one bit of good news,' he said, Doctor Knowles said a small tot of whisky at bedtime would do me good.' 'Did he give you a prescription?' asked Elsie. 'What! for whisky? Pull the other one.' 'I thought,' Ned continued in a wheedling tone, 'maybe you could get me some when you go to the shops.' 'Pull the other one' said Elsie.

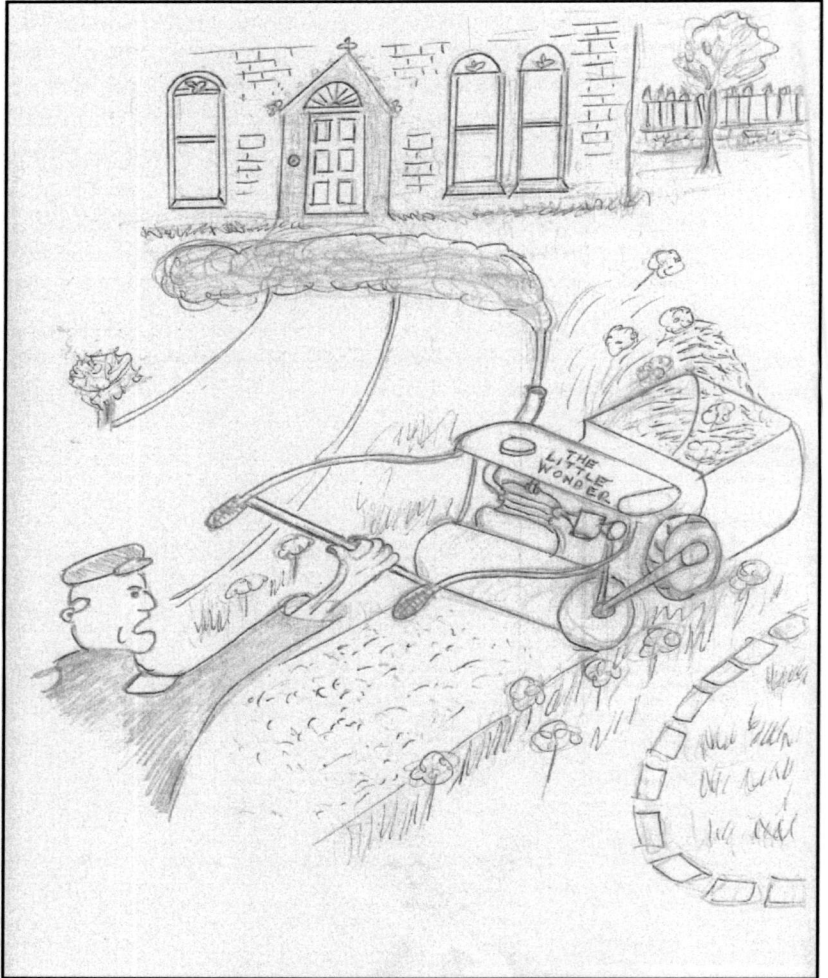

Straight through the flower bed

'The Gardener'

Uncle Ned had, since his retirement from shipbuilding, become used to a daily routine of visiting the pub or the betting shop or both. This routine had the inevitable effect of reducing his pocket money almost to zero. He then spent some time looking for casual work despite the fact that some work of this sort had lasted him a remarkably short time. He asked his friends for any information that might lead to any sort of opportunity.

'Why don't you volunteer for one of them charities that help old people with no money?' suggested Charlie the postman. 'Oh, aye, doing what?' asked Ned, suspecting that Charlie was making a sly joke at his expense. 'Collecting clothes or serving in the shop,' replied Charlie. 'What do you get for that?' asked Ned. 'Satisfaction,' replied Charlie. 'Satisfaction?' repeated Ned, scornfully 'how much ale does that buy?'

'Well, I might be able to help you' said Charlie, 'there's a gardener wanted at Swan House.' 'I ain't sure,' I mean, I never 'ad a garden.' replied Ned. 'If you want the job, go and see Mrs Henderson and try to convince her you are a gardener,' said Charlie impatiently.

The next day Ned went once more in search of work. Charlie's directions led him up the hill towards what had been a better-class district until it became run down. Swan House was one of the worst in that respect, it's blackened stonework stood almost hidden in several acres of neglected garden. Struggling past an overgrown bush half blocking the gate, Ned went up the crumbling drive and rang the bell. There was a long delay. He rang again.

The lady who opened the door was old, propped on two sticks, yet had an air of authority. The bleak stare she gave Ned after his introductory, 'Ello, luv,' would have stopped an avalanche. 'Whatever you are selling, I don't want any,' she said, closing the door. 'Ang on luv, I mean Madam,' said Ned. 'Charlie the postman sent me. He said you wanted a gardener.' The door creaked open a few inches. 'All right, I do need a gardener. Do you have any references?' Ned shook his head, 'Oh, never mind.' Said the lady, 'Have you done any gardening?' ' I 'ad an allotment once' replied Ned, not mentioning that he had failed to grow anything but weeds. 'That is most interesting,' said the lady, 'my late husband was Chairman of the Parks and Gardens Committee, Alderman Henderson.' 'What 'im,' exclaimed Ned "E got me chucked off me allotment.' 'What? what did you say?' asked the lady, who, fortunately for Ned, seemed to be a trifle deaf. 'He got me the allotment,' replied Ned.

'Well' said the lady decisively,' I'll give you a trial. You can begin by cutting the lawn. There's a mower in the shed. I take it you can use one?' Ned looked at the overgrown lawn and almost gave up. 'Aven't a clue,' he muttered.' 'What?' said the lady. 'I know what to do,' he replied, touching his flat cap.

The mower was huge and ancient. Faded gold lettering on the petrol tank proclaimed it, 'The Little Wonder.' It smelled of oil. Ned dragged it out from the shed and wondered what to do next. He found the petrol tap and turned it on. He turned the starting handle several times without any response apart from a gurgling noise in the machine and a gasping noise from Ned.

Unwilling to admit defeat, Ned hitched his wide leather belt, spat on his hands and tried again. There was a loud backfire and a thumping noise that gradually increased until the machine, vibrating wildly lurched toward the lawn. Ned tried to turn it as it ploughed through an overgrown flower border. 'Ow d'yer stop it?' yelled Ned. The machine then roared across the lawn, throwing grass cuttings in all directions. Ned realised that he had to solve the problem himself, he thought, if it runs on petrol, why not turn the tap off?

Staggering behind the machine as it crossed the lawn once more, he managed to turn the petrol off. His relief was short-lived; the machine did not stop. If anything it went faster, almost shaking Ned off altogether. It headed straight for the front door of the house, stopping at the last second before crashing through. There was an ear-splitting backfire. Ned was flung forward onto the steps just as Mrs Henderson opened the door.

'What are you doing down there, you stupid man,' she said, very sharply. 'Sweepin' the steps with me bum,' replied Ned . 'What?' she said. 'Just about got it done,' he said. 'It's not very neat,' said Mrs Henderson. 'You've cut it diagonally and then in circles, anything but the striped effect I require.' Ned struggled to his feet. 'I can't do no better, lady,' he said. 'What's that?' said Mrs Henderson. 'You say you can do better? How about clearing the pond?' 'I can't swim,' said Ned.

'What can you do?' said Mrs Henderson, 'can you do topiary? Ned looked puzzled. 'What's topiary?' he asked. Ignoring this, Mrs Henderson said, 'I want that bush by the gate trimmed into the shape of a swan, just as it was when my husband was alive. The Parks and Gardens workmen used to trim it every week.'

'I bet they did,' muttered Ned, gazing at the shapeless mass of greenery. He knew when to quit. 'Sorry ma,' he said shaking his head. 'Oh very well,' said Mrs Henderson huffily, 'If you don't want the job, here's a pound for what you've done.' 'You're very generous, said Ned ironically. 'Yes I am,' agreed Mrs Henderson. 'My husband used to say that if you give the lower classes an inch they'll take a mile. I'm not at all satisfied with your work. I shall have to speak to constable Stoat.' 'What for?' asked Ned, alarmed. 'I ain't broke the law.'

'No, no,' said Mrs Henderson, 'he said he had a young man in his charge who is doing community service.' A thought occurred to Ned. 'What's his name?' he asked. 'I think the Constable said his name was Head.' replied Mrs Henderson.' 'I thought so,' exclaimed Ned, 'it's Richard.' 'I don't think so,' Mrs Henderson replied, 'his name's 'er Darren, yes, that's it, Darren Head.' Ned shook his head. 'Them that knows 'im call him Richard. If you take me advice, lady, you won't let him through the gate.' 'Non-sense,' snapped Mrs Henderson. 'It's very commendable of him to do community service, very public spirited indeed. I'm sure I shall get on very well with the young man and I'm also sure that he will prove to be more satisfactory than a useless pensioner.'

Ned pocketed his pound and headed towards the 'Boilermakers Arms'. 'Best o' luck, lady,' he said. The following week Ned happened to pass Swan House. As he expected, Mrs Henderson and Richard had not struck up any great friendship. That was apparent from the sight of the bush by the gate. It was cut in a huge 'V'.

The large woman embraces Ned

'Open on Sundays'

Auntie Elsie was in a disgruntled mood. She glared at Ned across the breakfast table. Ned lowered his newspaper. 'What's wrong, love?' he enquired mildly. 'I'll tell you what's wrong,' she said, 'you're not fit to be seen, and on a Sunday and all.'

Ned pulled up his dangling braces and buttoned up his collarless shirt. 'Nobody comes 'ere so what does it matter?' he said. 'It matters to me,' replied Elsie angrily. Ned rose slowly from the table, put on his donkey jacket and moved towards the door.

'Where do you think you're going?' said Elsie, 'that disgraceful pub again?' 'That's just where you're wrong.' said Ned. 'Where then?' Elsie persisted. 'Church,' replied Ned over his shoulder as he went, leaving Elsie speechless with astonishment.

Ned had not been joking. He did go to church, or more accurately, to chapel, as the little red brick building had been called for as long as Ned could remember. Recently it had closed and had been saved from demolition or conversion to business premises by a religious group, new to the district, but known for a lively style of worship that attracted a large following.

Ned, whose attendances at places of worship were very infrequent to say the least had gone to the chapel at the request of Charlie the postman who was concerned that the pensioners in the new flats were getting isolated and needed more outside interests. He wanted Ned to attend a service at the chapel to find out if it would be suitable.

Lacking Charlie's concern for helping the elderly and disadvantaged, Ned was tempted to ask Charlie why he did not go to the chapel himself but, having accepted several free pints of beer from Charlie, decided that he ought to do something in return. In any case, he told himself, it would be interesting to see how the chapel had changed since his own attendances there at the Sunday school long ago.

The chapel was gloomy except for some flashing lights near the front. A music group was tuning up their instruments. There was no sign of the old organ that used to dominate the chapel when it was played loudly by an organist who played for the local cinema on weekdays. There were few seats left empty; they were filled mostly by young people. Ned almost fell over a pile of shopping bags as he sat near a large woman in a brightly-coloured dress like a flowery tent.

At least, thought Ned, there were a few older people attending the service, including the lady he was seated beside. 'Been shopping?' he enquired. 'Yes, why not?' she replied. 'Isn't there something in the Bible about keeping the Sabbath holy?' he said. 'You worked in the shipyard, didn't you?' she asked, 'Yes' replied Ned. 'How did you guess?' He removed his cap belatedly and shuffled his heavy boots. 'You worked overtime on Sundays didn't you?' asked the woman. 'Sometimes I 'ad to,' replied Ned. 'There was a war on.' 'There's a war on here too, against the Devil' she replied.

'What 'appened to the pews?' Ned asked, changing the subject. 'Gone,' she replied. 'Some of them went to that new beer garden down by the river. We don't want them. They get in the way of the dancing.' 'You mean dancing during the service?' asked Ned in astonishment. 'Things 'ave changed.'

Before the woman revealed any more shocks, the service began. It was led by a young man in casual dress. Ned was relieved to find that the prayers were recognisable and even the sermon was not very different from what he remembered except that there was a question and answer session when the congregation clamoured noisily to give answers. The hymns were very different from what Ned remembered, much louder and played very fast by the music group. They were not even called hymns; they were called songs. Ned tried to sing but soon became breathless. The congregation began to stamp and clap. Some even danced in the aisle.

Things became quieter when the time came for the collection. The lights dimmed and several collectors moved among the seats with large collecting bags. Ned, feeling slightly intimidated, handed over his loose change. The service ended with a benediction that the whole congregation was asked to chant after which people milled about, embracing each other. Ned, caught up in a bone-crushing embrace by the woman he had sat next to, found himself out on the pavement. With true survivor's instinct, he headed for the 'Boilermakers Arms.'

To Ned's surprise, Charlie was calmly drinking a pint of bitter. 'Where were you?' he asked. 'Ow d'you mean?' replied Charlie. 'I mean you asked me to go to that chapel and 'ere you are, boozin', said Ned. 'You could 'ave gone yourself.' Charlie said, a trifle guiltily, 'Sunday's me only day off.' 'Hard luck,' said Ned. 'Anyway,' said Charlie, passing a pint across, 'you're judgement's better than mine. Didn't you used to go that chapel when you were a kid? How do you think the pensioners from the flats would like it?'

Ned took a long swig from his pint. 'It might come as a bit of a shock,' he said. 'Didn't you tell me you used to enjoy going there?' persisted Charlie. Ned drained his glass and looked at it reflectively. 'I did enjoy it, he said. We played football in the winter and cricket in the summer. We 'ad a party at Christmas and an outing in a charabanc once a year.'

'Why did you pack it in?' asked Charlie. 'Well you know,' replied Ned, suddenly embarrassed, 'you get different interests when you start growing up.' 'What sort of interests?' persisted Charlie. 'If you really want to know,' replied Ned in an exasperated tone. 'They wanted me to sign the pledge.'

Mr Denham takes Charge

'The Old Comrade'

One day in November, Uncle Ned went for one of his slow aimless walks. It was sunny but cold, typical weather for early November. Ned pulled down the peak of his flat cap and pulled up the collar of his donkey jacket. He passed the betting shop (with an effort), passed the strangely silent sheds of the closed shipyard, until he came to a place known as the paddock. It was a small patch of rough grass and weeds near to the park but not actually part of it. It was frequented by elderly men who spent all day sitting on a low wall, studying racing papers. They were all experts and they were all broke.

Many of the men were even older than Ned, among them was 'Big Norman' a local hard man who could, in his prime, silence a pub by merely walking into it. He did not look very terrifying in old age, hunched over his paper.

Ned had a horror of ending up in such a group. Since his retirement he had tried to find a part-time occupation mainly without success. 'Never mind, eh.' Was his usual response. He walked on.

He came to a new block of flats, built recently as sheltered accommodation for pensioners. To his surprise Charlie the postman was entering the block. 'Bit late for delivering mail, isn't it?' said Ned. 'I've finished work,' said Charlie, 'this is me voluntary job, visiting lonely old people. You can come with me if you like.' 'Okay' agreed Ned, thinking it would be better than sitting in the paddock.

As they walked along the corridor Charlie explained that the

Secretary of the local British Legion had asked him to visit an old soldier, Mr Denham, to persuade him to come to a parade and reunion on Remembrance Sunday.

Charlie rapped at the door in an obviously pre-arranged way. There was a clatter of bolts and chains as the door was opened by a slim, grey-haired man with a military moustache. Ned was surprised at Mr Denham's smart appearance. The flat was clean and tidy, the living-room dominated by a full-length mirror. Charlie lost no time in asking Mr Denham to attend the Remembrance Day parade.

'I don't think so , sorry,' Mr Denham replied, 'I feel rather tired after looking out half the night in case the raiding parties came again.' 'Who?' asked Charlie, puzzled. 'I mean groups of youngsters causing trouble,' replied Mr Denham. 'Nothing to do,' put in Ned, 'a few weeks as a shipyard apprentice'd sort them out.' 'National Service is what they want,' said Charlie.

'During the war I had a revolver,' said Mr Denham. 'You haven't still got it, have you?' asked Charlie, alarmed. 'No, unfortunately, I threw it in the Rhine just before I was captured.' 'Don't talk like that,' said Charlie with a shudder, 'call the Police if you're scared.' 'I've tried it,' said Mr Denham, 'they do their best but by the time they get here the culprits have gone. As for being scared, I felt safer in a prisoner of war camp.'

On the way out Charlie said to Ned. 'I'm worried about 'im. He hardly ever goes out. A day out marching with the Army Cadets, the Girl Guides and any war veterans we can contact would do him a power of good. I'll see if I can change his mind before the weekend.'

When Ned arrived home Elsie placed a bowl of soup before him. 'Got the recipe from the Townswomen's Guild' she announced proudly, 'asparagus soup with croutons.' 'Great, love,' replied Ned, poking it dubiously 'apart from all these bits of hard bread.' 'Where've you been?' said Elsie in a sharper tone. 'I've been visiting,' Ned replied. 'What? a prison?' asked Elsie. 'No, the old people's flats,' Ned said. 'I'm a social worker now, a voluntary one anyway. I'm 'elping Charlie.' 'Well,' said Elsie, pleasantly surprised, 'that's an improvement on what you usually do with Charlie. I mean drinking or working on his old relic of a car.'

A few days later Ned went with Charlie to the Royal British Legion Remembrance Day Parade. 'I had another word with Mr Denham,' said Charlie, 'it cost me the price of a whisky and soda, but I think he'll come.'

When they got to the town square the parade was forming up for the march to the war memorial. Mr Denham was conspicuous at the front with medals pinned across his chest, a bowler hat square on his head and a furled umbrella carried at the slope. He tapped his watch. 'Marching off in ten minutes,' he said briskly, 'Look sharp.'

There followed an eventful hour when Mr Denham took command of the non-uniformed squad and marched them to the war memorial. Charlie, shuffling along in his RAF blazer, was harangued to 'get in step'. His efforts to do so resembled a hop, skip and jump. Ned wisely kept among the onlookers.

On return to the Legion Headquarters where a light lunch was provided, Mr Denham entertained everyone with a story of how he had caught a burglar at his flat the previous night. 'Stalked the beggar with a kitchen broom,' he said, holding his umbrella like a bayonet. 'He got in through the kitchen window, must have thought I was asleep. I crept up behind him.' 'What happened then?' somebody asked. 'He caught sight of me in the mirror, gave him a hell of a fright. He jumped clean out of the window.' 'Blimey,' said Ned, 'he's on the top floor.'

During the lunch a few pints had come Ned's way and by the time he got home he was slightly the worse for wear. 'Where've you been?' asked Elsie, recognising the signs, 'helping old people again?' Ned slumped down on the settee. 'I'll 'ave to give this social work up.' he muttered, 'it's too frightening.'

Big Norman wins the argument

'A Day at the Seaside'

One morning in November, Ned was strolling in the park enjoying the mild, sunny weather. He paused by the bowling green where a group of his contemporaries were engaged in an apparently friendly, but in fact quite vicious game of bowls. He became aware of heavy breathing behind him. 'I've been looking for you,' said Charlie the postman. 'What d'you want doing this time?' said Ned. 'It's not what I want, it's the old folks in the flats and in Willowbrook House. They usually have a day out at the seaside this time of year when it's quieter, but the driver of the minibus has gone off sick.' 'Can't you get another driver?' asked Ned. 'Can you drive?' asked Charlie. 'No, only 'orses,' said Ned. 'Well, in that case I'll have to do it. You can come with me.' 'What's it going to cost?' asked Ned suspiciously. 'Nothing,' said Charlie, 'so long as you help with the supervision.' 'Thought there'd be a catch' muttered Ned. 'You might get a free beer or two' said Charlie. 'When do we start?' asked Ned.

On the morning of the outing, the fine autumn weather was still holding. The minibus, with Charlie at the wheel was ready to go. Inside were the two groups of pensioners. The ones from the Home, including Methylated Maggie and Big Norman had the assistant Matron, Lavinia, as their supervisor. She was already flustered. Known to the residents as Vinegar, she tried hard to be firm, declaring that her boss, the Matron was 'too kind.' The group from the flats was unsupervised but Mr Denham appeared to have taken charge of them.

They arrived without incident at the seaside where a light lunch had been arranged at one of the numerous cafes. After lunch the groups began to disperse in spite of the assistant Matron's efforts to keep them together. Mr Denham declared quite openly that he was going for a drink. Methylated Maggie, who had been very subdued all morning brightened up and followed him like a terrier. Big Norman was seen shambling in the same direction.

The assistant Matron was completely distracted. 'They don't listen to me at all,' she complained. 'I can't go and keep an eye on them and leave these others here'. "These others", the less mobile residents of the Home, were settling down on the benches along the promenade to enjoy the sun.

'I can't leave the minibus' said Charlie. 'It's on a no-parking place and if a traffic warden comes along I've got to explain it's for disabled people.' They both looked at Ned. 'I'll go to the pub,' he said, rising to the occasion, 'and make sure they don't get into no trouble.' Unfortunately, by the time Ned set off, the group of pensioners had turned off the promenade into one of the many side streets. Ned had to visit several pubs before he found the right one.

Mr Denham, by then under the influence of a few whisky and sodas, was a more commanding presence than ever. He introduced Ned to a seedy looking individual in a stained blazer. 'This is Bert,' he said, 'ex-artillery – served right through the desert campaigns.'

Big Norman who, like Ned had worked in the shipyard all through the war, was not impressed by the military talk. He poured scorn on the desert campaigns and said he'd seen more fighting at home. Given Norman's record as a bruiser, probably this was true.

Bert, to his credit was not intimidated by the big man and the argument got more heated. Maggie, laughing shrilly at every remark, sided with Norman and began to tell how she was bombed out of house and home. Her tale was interrupted when Bert began prodding Big Norman in the chest, which was very unwise.

Ignoring Mr Denham's, 'steady on chaps!', Norman caught Bert with a left hook to the right ear that sent him staggering along the bar, scattering glasses in all directions. Bert showed true veteran's courage by lunging back at Norman. Although not apparent to Bert, the big man was unsteady on his legs. He sprawled flat on his back over a table, sending everything crashing into the doorway. 'Get out,' yelled the barman, 'out, the lot of you. Flippin' pensioners – and they try to tell you it's the youngsters who cause all the trouble.'

By the time Ned got his charges back to the minibus, the assistant Matron, alias 'Vinegar' was frantic with anxiety. She calmed down when she realised that the dishevelled and beer-stained Norman had not suffered any real harm. She was less interested in Mr Denham and his friend who were not in her charge. Mr Denham was trying to tell Norman he ought to have more respect for an old soldier. Norman in return was giving Mr Denham a few words of advice – very rude words.

Methylated Maggie seemed much her usual self except for a tendency to cackle with laughter and break into song from time to time. She entertained all present with her repertoire of old songs which she sang very well apart from occasionally slurring the words.

The following day Ned was pleased to receive a few free pints of beer from Charlie in return for services rendered, but he made a point of saying he would not be keen to repeat the experience. 'Not much fear of that,' said Charlie. 'I've just been up to Willowbrook House with the mail. The Matron told me I shouldn't have let any of them go into a pub. I tried to tell her I was only the driver. She told me that was my good fortune. When I saw Lavinia later I saw what she meant, poor 'Vinegar' looked like she'd been crying half the night.'

To add the trouble they had to get the doctor to Maggie. They thought she was dying.' 'And was she?' asked Ned. 'Nah,' said Charlie, 'just a case of terminal hangover.'

Ned stops the leak

'The Instant Plumber'

Uncle Ned returned home after attending a funeral. Auntie Elsie had not wanted him to go, partly because of the likelihood of him partaking too freely of the hospitality that usually follows such events, and partly because she wanted him to repair a water leak in the outside toilet. However, to Elsie's surprise, he had come home both promptly and sober.

The funeral was that of an old man who had run a scrap wood business for more years than most people in the district could remember. Elsie had forgotten that the old man had been Ned's first employer, and Ned, crass though he appeared at times, had feelings of respect. 'He must have been very old,' said Elsie, 'he used to be called the old man when I was a girl and used to go out with the pawnbroker's son, a lad who knew how to dress.'

'Some people 'ave got to have a what d'you call it, an image,' said Ned, aware that he was once again being compared to Elsie's first fiancé. In the silence that followed, Elsie inspected Ned's appearance. It was obvious from her expression that she did not approve of his brown chalk-stripe suit, shrunken since he fell into a canal wearing it, nor did she like his heavy black boots. He had left off his customary flat cap and his bald head had gone a fine shade of mauve.

'Hope you didn't catch cold in that graveyard,' said Elsie. 'It wasn't a burial, it was a cremation – quite 'ot as a matter of fact,' replied Ned. 'I've never been to a crematorium,' said Elsie, 'What's it like?' 'Charlie said it was like an airport – with departures only.' 'He would say that,' said Elsie, scornfully. Shaking her head with irritation, she switched on the television and began changing channels with the remote control, It was a new set, their first with a remote control. Elsie had saved for it out of her pension and was very proud of it, and slightly intimidated, She held the control unit at arm's length like someone firing a flare and jumped visibly every time the picture changed. 'He died of pleasure,' Ned said suddenly, 'Who?' asked Elsie, dropping the control unit. 'The old man,' said Ned, 'he went to Blackpool last week with his granddaughter. He'd never had a holiday before and he went on the big dipper.'

'Poor old man,' said Elsie. 'I remember him walking around with his old dog, that big mastiff, it was his guard dog.' 'It was too old to guard anything,' said Ned, 'it's back legs were all bent. Charlie said it looked like a hyena.' 'That's not a nice thing to say' said Elsie, 'It's a pity Charlie never took up a proper profession, and you too.' 'Do you mean pawnbroking?' said Ned. 'At least me fiance knew how to treat a girl,' she said, 'I've still got one of his presents, a bottle of toilet water.' 'Blimey, that's not much,' said Ned, 'give me a jug and I'll get you some more.' 'Where from?' asked Elsie. 'From the toilet,' replied Ned. 'While you are there, fix that pipe,' said Elsie with a clear message of finality. Ned went into the backyard and rummaged in a small shed that had once been a packing case. He took out what looked like a small sledge hammer with a long flexible shaft. It was a riveting hammer. Flexing it like a golf club, he advanced on the toilet.

Elsie heard a series of rapid thuds before Ned, slightly out of breath returned to the living room. 'That was quick,' remarked Elsie in astonishment. 'It won't leak no more,' assured Ned. 'What did you do?' asked Elsie. 'Bashed the pipe flat,' replied Ned, heading for the door. His final remark left Elsie open-mouthed and speechless. 'I couldn't 'ave done that if I'd been a pawnbroker.'

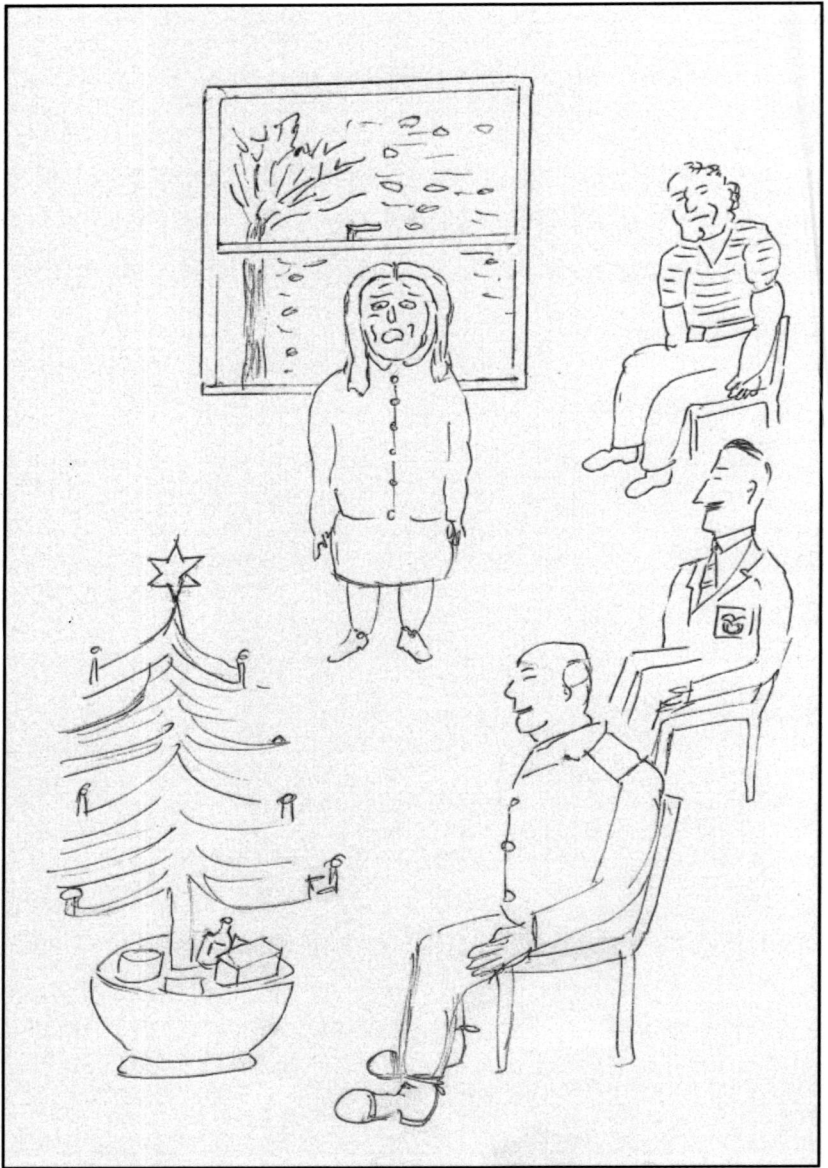

Maggie's Solo

'Christmas Day at the Retirement Home'

Uncle Ned stood at the bar of the 'Boilermakers Arms' next to Charlie the postman. Outside it was a cold day, bleak, on the run-up to Christmas. 'Have another pint,' said Charlie. 'Ta very much,' replied Ned, wondering what was behind Charlie's generosity this time. 'What's worrying you?' he asked. 'Willowbrook House.' Charlie replied. 'I thought you 'ad enough to worry about at the old peoples' flats' said Ned. 'I 'ave,' replied Charlie, 'what with that old soldier, Mr Denham, forming a vigilante group and going out at night trying to catch burglars and vandals.'

Charlie waited a moment until Ned's glass was almost empty, then he said, 'will you do something for me?' 'What?' asked Ned, warily. 'Go to Willowbrook House and help out at the residents' Christmas party.' Ned almost choked. 'Why can't you do it? I mean you'll be on your own anyway. I've got a wife who'll be expecting me to spend some time with her. You do-gooders are all the bloomin' same. You take on more than you can cope with and then expect everybody else to help you out.'

'I've got to help out at the flats, somebody's got to help the old folks,' said Charlie, 'we'll all be old some day.' He looked pointedly at Ned who had retired from work at the shipyard a few years previously. 'All right, I'll do it,' said Ned. 'Stout feller', said Charlie, 'have another pint.'

Christmas Day dawned bright and cold. 'Frost's cracking the

flags,' said Ned, putting on his donkey jacket and flat cap. 'Where are you going to this Christmas morning?' asked Auntie Elsie, disappointed at not getting a present from Ned. 'To Willowbrook House,' replied Ned, 'to entertain the old folks.' 'That should be worth seeing,' said Elsie, surprised that he was going to do something useful instead of getting drunk.

Willowbrook House was in a state of turmoil. The Matron, usually calm and steady, was near to panic. 'Some of the relatives came in with bottles and handed them round before I could stop them. I'm trying to get the Christmas dinner ready with one young girl to help. The rest of the staff's not turned in.' 'What d'you want me to do?' asked Ned. 'Go into the lounge and calm them down,' was the reply.

The lounge was in an uproar. A carol service was on the television. Some of the residents were joining in the singing. When 'O Come All Ye Faithful' came on, they sang, 'Why are we waiting?' 'Quiet please,' called Ned, feeling like a hopeless teacher faced with an uncontrollable class. There was no response. Methylated Maggie, looking amazingly clean, conducted the others like a choirmaster.

Ned tried to tell some jokes. 'Does anyone know the difference between a potato masher and a sink plunger? You don't madam? then I'm not coming to your 'ouse for dinner.' There was not much response except that someone shouted, 'Shut your face.' 'Did you go to the football last Saturday?' bawled Ned. 'I didn't go myself. They never come to see me when I'm in a bad way.' Again there was no response. 'Can anybody do a turn? Asked Ned, desperately. 'I can play the spoons,' offered a man seated in the corner. 'I can sing,' said Maggie. 'I'll get some spoons,' said Ned, darting into the kitchen.

The Matron was now assisted by another woman. 'My prayers are answered,' said the Matron. 'The cook turned up. We'll serve dinner shortly. Everything alright in the lounge? 'Yeah,' lied Ned, taking the spoons.

When he returned to the lounge, the television was switched off and Maggie was singing. It was an old song, 'The Brown Bird', and Maggie was hitting every note clear and true. There was silence until she finished, then loud applause. The Matron came in to announce that the meal was ready. 'Where did you learn to sing like that, Maggie?' she asked. 'Ere,' was the reply. The Matron shrugged in a puzzled manner, then announced that dinner was ready. She asked Ned to stay for dinner but Ned said, 'Thanks, but me missus will 'ave made me dinner.' 'Well Ned, Christmas is for the family after all.' said the Matron. 'Aye, so it is,' said Ned, thinking of all the drunken Christmases and spoilt dinners he'd caused. The Matron shook his hand. 'God bless you Ned, and a happy Christmas to you.' It was colder than ever as Ned walked down the drive. In his mind he could hear the high, ringing notes of Maggie's song. Fine snow was blowing in the wind. It got in his eyes a bit and made them water.

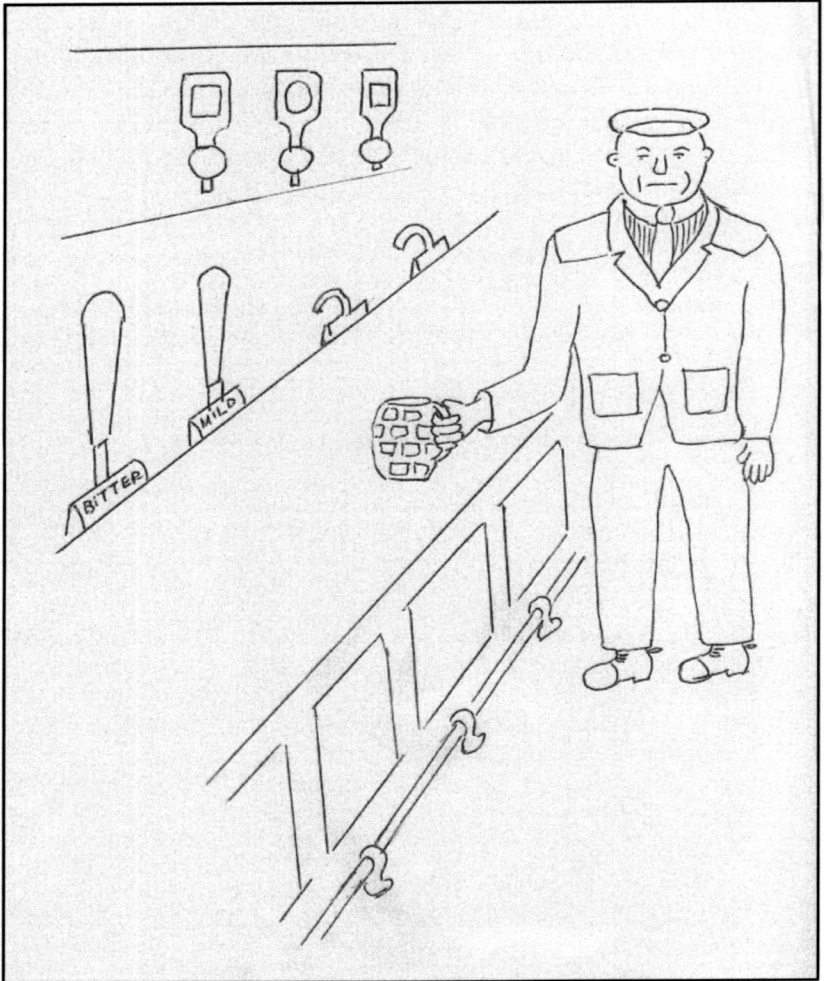

A really great man

'Uncle Ned looks back'

Auntie Elsie was behaving peculiarly, according to Uncle Ned that is. 'Would you like another croissant?' she asked at breakfast, 'or some toast with low fat spread?' 'I wouldn't mind some sausage and fried bread,' said Ned. 'Now you know fry-ups aren't good for you. They told us at the Townswomen's Guild.' 'B-bother the bloomin' Guild,' he said. 'See, you're stammering already,' replied Elsie. 'What's your blood pressure like?' 'Rising,' he said. 'Why are you worrying about me 'ealth all of a sudden?' 'I want you to last a bit longer,' she said, 'It's your birthday, you're seventieth,' said Elsie, It's your three score years and ten, your lifespan.' 'Ow d'you figure that out?' said Ned 'It's in the Bible.' replied Elsie.

'From now on,' said Elsie, 'you're going to live a healthier lifestyle. You can start straight away by washing the backyard. As Ned threw buckets of water onto the stone flags, he thought of the changes in domestic life that had taken place since his father's time. He shook his head. In them days a man was boss in his own house. 'Talking to yourself now?' asked Elsie, suddenly appearing at the door, 'Eh?' said Ned, swinging around and accidentally spilling a bucketful of water over Elsie's feet.

'If it wasn't your birthday, I'd jam that bucket over yer 'ead.' Elsie's veneer of culture, acquired at the Guild, slipped easily. Ned did not retaliate. He had learned the value of discretion over the years since his first Christmas with Elsie as a newly-married couple. Ned had behaved in the way most of the older men behaved whenever there was a holiday. He went out and got drunk. He came in very late for his Christmas dinner, a roast goose that his new bride had gone to considerable trouble to prepare. It did not look very appetising in its dried-up state, nor did Ned feel much inclined to eat it, considering the amount of beer he had drunk.

True to tradition, he declared that the goose was overcooked and was not fit for a dog to eat. He then threw it down the backyard and, for good measure, cuffed his new bride across the ear, just to show who was boss. Instead of bursting into apologetic tears, as Ned expected, Elsie made the grim remark, 'You've just cooked your goose'. She then threw Ned down the yard, following the dinner.

It had taken Ned a while to work out why he, a young hard man who had settled more than a few arguments down at the shipyard with his fists, was now lying in a tangled heap. He knew now. Looking at Elsie's forearms, folded across her apron, he could see they were like bars of teak.

'I've just finished, love,' he said. 'I think I might go for a drink, seeing it's me birthday.' 'Don't get drunk.' Said Elsie, 'and don't be late. I've got a treat planned for your birthday. We're going to the theatre.' She showed him the tickets, "When we are Married," by J. B. Priestley.

More bloomin' culture, he thought. At least it can't be worse than that orchestral concert we went to last year. The fuss she made when I remarked, 'Is that the best they can play?' How was I to know they were tuning up? The other night she said she had been studying a letter written in French by someone called Zola. I'd never heard of her, nor the feller it was all about, Jack Hughes.

Entering the 'Boilermakers Arms' was, in a way, like coming home. Charlie was at the bar boring 'Arry Wade with his car problems. Ned sipped at his pint and related the events of the trip to the seaside. I heard about it, 'said 'Arry. 'That big thug got his comeuppance,' he said cheerfully. 'Mind you', said Ned, 'he hasn't been the same since they took the cartridges out of his knees.' Charlie looked round at Ned, 'Have another pint?' Ned's face contorted with the inner struggle. 'No, thanks, I got to go. I can't let Elsie down, she's got tickets for a play called 'Let's get married or something.'

'Not like him to refuse a drink,' remarked Charlie after Ned had left. 'I've never known it before,' agreed 'Arry. 'He's a right character,' said Charlie. 'Aye, daft as a brush,' said 'Arry. 'I dunno,' said Charlie. 'He's got some good qualities.' 'Like what?' asked 'Arry, eyebrows raised. 'Well,' replied Charlie, 'sometimes I think he's got a touch of greatness.' 'This ale must be stronger than I thought,' said 'Arry, grinning.

'Let me explain,' said Charlie, seriously, 'he's got a lot of faults, right?' 'Right' said 'Arry. 'But for one thing he's loyal,' continued Charlie, 'he doesn't go calling people behind their backs. It's easy to be great if you're good at everything. Ned's got his faults but he can carry them faults and people still look up to him. That, in my opinion, is what makes a truly great man.'